# Bad Business

## Billionaire's Club #17

## Elise Faber

BAD BUSINESS
BY ELISE FABER
Newsletter sign-up

BAD BUSINESS
Copyright © 2023 Elise Faber
Print ISBN-13: 978-1-63749-110-2
Ebook ISBN-13: 978-1-63749-109-6

# BILLIONAIRE'S CLUB

Bad Night Stand

Bad Breakup

Bad Husband

Bad Hookup

Bad Divorce

Bad Fiancé

Bad Boyfriend

Bad Blind Date

Bad Wedding

Bad Engagement

Bad Bridesmaid

Bad Swipe

Bad Girlfriend

Bad Best Friend

Bad Rebound

Bad Romance

Bad Business

# ONE

## ROME

"I hate you!"

"I—"

Before I could finish the sentence, the door slammed in my face, missing my fingers by an inch, my forehead by less.

I'd had experience in getting doors slammed on me.

A *lot* of experience in the last year.

Hence, I knew exactly where to keep my hands and head so they were out of harm's way.

Sighing, I turned away, walking down the hall, down the stairs, and heading straight for the fridge.

And the beer.

I needed a *fucking* beer considering my brain had started throbbing about midway through the argument. I knew it wouldn't stop. Not so long as my life was this fucked up.

It had taken three long years to get Jack here.

And in the three hundred and forty-seven days since my son had moved into my house, I'd made zero progress in breeching the gulf between us.

And...I was starting to think it was hopeless.

Hence the throbbing in my fucking temples.

Hence the need for a fucking beer.

Unfortunately, I had just reached the landing and turned for the kitchen, for the fridge, for that beer when someone knocked at the door.

"Fuck," I muttered, debating the likelihood of successfully ignoring the intrusion.

The problem was that it was likely one of my brothers or one of my brothers' wives, or my *mother*, and ignoring wouldn't do shit.

They'd just barge their way in and make themselves at home.

Jack would sure as shit prefer that.

He couldn't stand me, couldn't fucking *stand me*.

I understood why.

I'd ruined his life.

But...he loved my family.

The knock came again, and I ground my teeth together, preparing to swallow my pride in the hope that whichever Hutchins had come knocking would be able to smooth things over with Jack.

I was getting really tired of hearing my son tell me that he hated me.

Lamenting that my beer consumption—and look, I may be fixated on the beer in this moment, but it would only be one, I wouldn't fuck with my kid's life that way—would be delayed, I stifled a sigh and moved to answer the door, my hand barely reaching the knob before the knock came a third time.

Softer now, as though the person on the other side wanted to make their presence known, but without disturbing me.

Mel, then.

Perfect.

Jack loved my brother's soft-spoken wife.

Probably because she was one of the nicest people on the planet.

I turned the knob, tugged open the door...

And standing on the other side of it, waiting there on my porch, was a woman I hadn't seen in four years.

"Maddie," I whispered.

Her mouth turned up. "Hey, Ro."

# Two

MADDIE

I was sitting on a barstool in Rome's house.

After four years abroad, managing the new—well, not so new *now*—European division of Ash's multibillion dollar company, it felt strange.

To be in the States.

To be in Rome's house.

To be sitting here and feeling my heart do that flutter again.

The one that had always been present with this man, the one I'd desperately ignored. Because that was what I did. Because I only tackled tasks I could control and...I would never be able to control this man.

Spreadsheets. Planning meetings. Handling tricky clients and frustrating manufacturing delays and even leaky freaking roofs —*those* I could manage.

The complication of relationships?

Not so much.

Of course, that was before I'd begun working for a Hutchins.

There was only so much a girl could do to avoid being swept

up into their lives. They were just so nice and welcoming and...pushy.

Pushy was written into the Hutchins' genetic code.

"Beer?" Ro asked, the slight rasp in his voice making me shiver.

I'd dreamed about that voice, dreamed about it so often I felt the question tickle up between my thighs, press against my clit, and—

"Maddie?"

Cheeks hot, I glanced up, met deep brown eyes. Ro had the *best* eyes—the color of dark chocolate with flecks of gold in those depths.

They were warm too.

Like that chocolate river in Willy Wonka.

Only *not* a river. And not dangerous.

A hot tub of melted chocolate...that wouldn't murder me.

He leaned back against the island next to me, two bottles of beer in one hand, the other lifting and cupping my jaw, tilting my head back so I got lost in those pools of liquidy, delicious chocolate. "You good?"

My cheeks flamed. "I'm good," I said quickly. "Just jet lagged and a little spacey." I leaned back slightly, enough for him to get the hint and release my jaw. Which, thankfully, he got, dropping his hand, and offering me one of the beers from his other.

I took it. "Thanks," I murmured, taking a sip.

A flash of a smile, but it wasn't bone deep, wasn't the mischievous Rome Smile I'd come to know.

Worry immediately began to churn in my gut.

"Is it Jack?" I asked softly, that sip of beer I'd taken sitting heavy in my stomach.

He'd been lifting his bottle toward his mouth but my question had him freezing. "What?"

"Is something wrong with Jack?" I asked. "Is that what put the look on your face?"

That beer dropped, foam sloshing up over the rim, sliding

down the side...and turning that churning in my stomach into full-on hundred-foot waves.

I hopped up, grabbed a paper towel, took the bottle, and wiped the sides. Then bent and swiped at the floor, cleaning up the drops that had made it that far. "Now," I said quietly. "What's going on?"

"What look on my face?" he asked, seemingly a question behind.

"The one that says you've been gut-punched when you were least expecting it."

He sucked in a breath, set the beer on the counter, and turned away from me.

Hundred-foot waves and a hurricane bearing down on us.

I moved around him, getting close enough to study his eyes.

He didn't make me work for it. "Jack's fine. Physically," he whispered. "Emotionally, though, he's a mess." Ro's head came up and he tried for his smile again, but I could tell it was total bullshit. Something his next words confirmed. "I tore him from everything he knew and brought him to a different country, inserted him into a new family." Ro shoved a hand through his hair, gaze going over my head. "I can't blame him for being pissed and hurt and scared, even after a year."

Rome's baby mama had pulled a disappearing act on him eight years before, and he'd found out he had a son just four years ago, after she died and Jack's custody fell into question.

Because Ro's name wasn't on the birth certificate and the person who'd mentioned it to Rome—an old friend of his and his fiancée that wasn't to be—the battle to just get a DNA test was rough, not to mention getting Jack here.

To the States.

How did I know this?

Even from my perch in Europe, I'd made many a phone call to lawyers and doctors and therapists, working my magic.

I was good at getting shit done.

I'd vowed that Jack wouldn't be left behind, that Rome wouldn't be left wondering.

And now...*I* wondered if that had been the wrong thing to do.

I'd always dreamed of a family and the thought of a three-year-old alone in the world, without people like the Hutchinses to take his back...

Motivated.

I'd been motivated to make sure he had a place where he felt at home.

Because I knew what it was like to *not* have that.

"But Ash said he's fitting right in with the family," I whispered.

Ro's mouth kicked up. "He *loves* my family. Asks to spend time with them regularly." A sigh. "It's *me* that he has a problem with."

Well...*shit*.

"Yeah," he murmured, clearly reading that off my face.

I tucked away old wounds, focused on what I could do now, what I could *fix* now.

That was what I did.

Fix things.

"What's going on?" I asked, passing him back his beer.

"Besides the whole being-ripped-from-his-family thing?"

That was a doozy.

But...

"Yeah," I said.

"He doesn't like that I have a bedtime for him." Ro sipped his beer then plunked it back onto the counter, counting off on his fingers. "Doesn't like that I make him finish his homework before he can go to soccer practice. Doesn't like that I make him introduce me to his friends' parents before he can play at their houses. He doesn't like"—Ro dropped his hand, went for his beer again—"me," he said on a sigh.

Shit.

This wasn't good.

It was very *not* good, and I needed to find a way to fix it.

For the little boy I'd never met in person, who I'd merely exchanged greetings and waves with over FaceTime. For the little boy who was innocent and deserved to understand his place in this world. For *Ro* who I—

"Oh."

I jerked, being the one who risked spilling my beer this time, and turned...

To see Jack standing in the doorway.

He was the spitting image of Rome. And seriously, watch out world. When Jack got older, he was going to be just as much of a heartbreaker as his dad was.

"You're not Mel," he pointed out, apparently not remembering my cool FaceTime waving abilities.

I supposed that wasn't unusual.

I'd made it an art form to exist in the background.

My lips tipped up. "No," I said. "Unfortunately, I'm not nearly as cool as Mel."

The little boy with golden-flecked brown eyes studied me for several long moments. Maybe seeing if I was being facetious, gauging my sincerity.

Either way, he seemed to judge and find me acceptable, moving closer and asking, "Who are you, anyway?"

Ro made a sound like he was going to interject—maybe because it wasn't the most polite of questions—but I figured that with things being so tense already, we didn't need to get into a confrontation about a semi-polite question.

Instead, I set down my beer, hopped to my feet, and walked over to Jack, sticking out my hand for him to shake. "I'm Maddie."

His head cocked to the side, those golden-brown eyes sliding over my shoulder and growing unfocused, as though he was trying to place my name. Then they flashed back to mine and held. "Ash's Maddie?"

I nodded. "Yeah."
"From FaceTime?"
I grinned.

# THREE

Ro

Why was it *not* a surprise that Jack and Maddie had hit it off?

I hadn't even been able to ask her what brought her to my doorstep before she'd arrowed in on my issues and set about solving them—the first something I'd experienced in my kitchen not two hours before, the second I knew from *past* experience.

Because she and her Maddie Magic were a big reason I had Jack here now.

But her magic was more than just navigating attorneys and court orders and running an entire division of my brother's company.

It was...bonding with my kid, who'd hated me from the first moment he'd laid eyes on me, navigating through the barbed wires and spikes, and earning genuine laughter and smiles. Swear to fuck, I hadn't even gotten a real smile for the first six months.

And now, I was leaning against the doorframe, pretending to not be watching them as they sat on the swings I'd had installed in my back yard.

Along with the play structure.

And the pool. And the hot tub.

And the landscaping and—

Hell, the house in general.

After Jack's mother had skipped out on our relationship in the middle of the night, ghosting me and leaving me wondering where in the fuck I'd gone so wrong, I'd been all in on condo life.

On *bachelor* life.

On working hard but not letting it take over my life.

Because I had done every-fucking-thing to make a perfect life and ensure a happy future for Carrie and I and the family I'd hoped to make with her.

And...that hadn't been enough to make her stay.

So, I might as well just...cut loose.

Live big and free and—

Maddie laughed again, louder this time.

I sighed.

That had worked out great, hadn't it?

A kid I hadn't known about. A dead baby mama. A custody battle that had raged on for years.

And now my life was a son who couldn't stand me...and work.

Because something had to be done to pay for the legal fight, for the house, for the swing set...for the pool.

Though, strictly speaking, the last had come from the unexpected surprise of my business taking off, my bank account growing to obscene proportions, and my suddenly finding myself as the head of a multibillion-dollar company.

No one was more shocked than me.

Free and loose to—

My phone rang.

To *this.*

I glanced away from Maddie and Jack on the swings, heart pulsing for a reason I didn't want to acknowledge and down at the screen, seeing that my assistant was calling.

Bonnie was amazing.

She wasn't what Maddie had been for my brother, ruling his life with an iron fist, showing such promise that Ash had felt comfortable promoting her over and over again (until she'd ended up as the COO of his European division), but Bonnie was still more than capable.

Sweet, matronly, the grandmother I'd always wished I'd had.

But her calling on a weekend meant that shit was hitting the fan.

I glanced from my cell, back up to the best buddies on the swings, and then down to my phone again.

I might as well get what was sure to be a painful conversation over with while Jack was occupied and happy.

Swiping across the screen, I lifted my cell up to my ear. "Bonnie."

"Ro," she said. "You're not going to like this."

I knew that shit was going down just from the timing of the call.

But I very much suspected that she was right—I wasn't going to like what Bonnie had to say.

Not one fucking bit.

I flicked one more look toward my son, toward Maddie, and walked down the hall, to the kitchen, leaning back against the island and bracing. "Lay it on me."

She did.

And, *fuck*, it was worse than I'd expected.

"No," I said, long minutes later, after Bonnie had looped in several of my VPs and stayed on the call to take notes, "that's not going to work. Do you want to fuck us on compliance? The share-holders alone will—"

A sound behind me had me whipping around.

Maddie froze in the doorway of the kitchen, hands coming up, palms out. "Sorry," she mouthed, starting to back out.

"Hang on," I said into the phone, hitting the button to mute my end of the call, and crossed to her. I captured her wrist before she slipped back out of the room, sparks shooting up my finger-tips, heat blooming in my palm. Even though I'd touched her before, it had never felt like this, and the contact, the heat, the way my cock reacted was...surprising. But before I could sit in that feeling, something else had worry clenching in my gut. "Is Jack okay?"

Her lips had parted, gaze unfocused, but my question had her eyes sharpening, returning to mine. "He's fine. I just came in to get us some water."

Oh.

"Right." I nodded, dropped her hand, and stepped back, feeling awkward because...

I didn't know why.

Even though it had been years since I'd seen her, this woman had been a fixture in my family for years. She'd spent time in my kitchen—not this one but at my bachelor pad—spent time in my brothers' houses and my mom's and—

*I'd* spent time with her.

But had I ever touched her?

Certainly. I *had* to have. And—right—I *had*. I'd done it just hours before.

I just never felt—

My cock never—

"You should get back to that call," Maddie said softly, tugging me out of my thoughts. "And if you have to go into the office, Jack and I will be fine."

"I—"

She went on, "I was heading over to Ash and Mel's anyway and he can tag along."

My lungs inflated and I held that air inside then slowly released it. "You don't have to—"

"I found my soccer ball, Maddie! Want to go play?"

She smiled at me, ordered softly, "Take the call. Jack and I will play. And if you have to go in, I'll bring him over to Ash and Mel's, yeah?"

Then, not giving me a chance to reply—probably because she knew there wouldn't be anything I would be able to say in return —she turned and met Jack in the hall. "I don't know the right way to kick one. Can you teach me?"

Jack glanced at me.

*I'd* been the one to show him that.

One of the few things he'd allowed me to give him.

But before I could sit in that feeling, he glanced back at Maddie. "I can teach you!" And then he ran down the hall, bursting out the back door—and slamming it in the process.

I sighed, looked up.

Maddie was watching me closely again.

"It'll be okay," she murmured, moving to the pad of paper I kept near the fridge, picking up the pen, and pulling out her phone. She tapped at the screen for a few moments then scribbled something onto the page. Nodding smartly, she tore off the sheet and walked back over to me, pressing it into my free hand. *"It'll be okay."*

I glanced down at the name and number on the page.

A name that was familiar, a connection that might help me through the shitshow on the phone.

More of Maddie's magic.

My eyes had barely scanned the paper, brain still processing what she'd given me, before she too was gone, her footsteps disappearing down the hall, the opening and closing of the back door barely audible.

Disquiet and relief sat heavy in my stomach, warring like the enemies they were.

But voices echoed loudly through the speaker of my cell, not giving me any time to sit in that, to process what the fuck was going on in my head, my body, my cock.

"Rome, you there?" Bonnie was asking.

Christ.

Work was calling.

Something I'd never thought would be my life.

But—my gaze went to the doorway through which Maddie had disappeared—a lot of things about my life were how I'd never expected them to be.

Sighing, I jabbed at the mute button, put it back up to my ear, and said, "Yeah, I'm here."

# Four

MADDIE

"These cheeks," I murmured, stroking a finger down the baby's downy soft skin. "I swear I've never seen anything like them."

Mel, her expression more content than Maddie had ever seen —something that probably had to do with the toddler running around the back yard, chasing Jack on chubby little legs and the tiny human I'd absconded with the moment I'd walked through the front door—smiled. "I don't know where she gets them."

Genetics were a fickle beast.

But I saw a lot of Mel in the two-month-old.

"I'm sorry I couldn't get here before she was born," I said softly, holding the baby close, committing every moment of this peaceful, gorgeous little one to memory.

I hadn't been back to California for a year, so freaking busy with work for the past few years that I barely knew what to do with myself now that things were set up and running effectively and didn't require every spare waking moment to make sure the wheels didn't fall off.

"You're here now," Mel said softly. "And you were Ash's eyes and ears and *savior* for the project, so I can't complain." She leaned in, nudged my shoulder with her own. "I missed you, though."

I had missed Mel too.

"Well, like you said"—I nudged her back, careful to not jostle the baby—"I'm here now."

"Yeah." A beat that spoke volumes. "And with Jack."

"I stopped by Rome's place," I admitted, not that it was a surprise, considering I'd arrived at my friend's house with his son in tow. "I wanted to check if he and Jack needed anything."

Mel tilted her head to the side, studying me.

"What?"

Another pause that spoke volumes, but to her credit, Mel didn't say anything...or anything about the fact that I'd arrived at her house with Jack in my back seat.

Though, that could be because the little peanut in my arms started to fuss.

Like the newborn mom she was, Mel had swept her out of my hold and was feeding her in approximately three-point-two seconds, and doing it with all the aplomb of an experienced mother. "So," she said once the baby had latched and was eating contentedly, "tell me about Europe."

"You know about Europe," I said lightly. "It's mostly work and very little play"—so little in fact that I had quite the dry streak going—"I want to hear more about you and the babies."

Mel—*still* the newborn (and toddler) mom that she was—obliged and I soaked in all the little moments she shared, the ones I'd missed witnessing firsthand because I'd moved to Europe, the ones I treasured because while I might be on the outskirts of the big, vociferous, *wonderful* family that were the Hutchinses, I still loved them all deeply.

Eventually, though, the baby finished eating and the stories petered out.

"Now," Mel said, passing the baby back, but this time with a burp cloth, just in case of leakage, "how did you end up with Jack?"

"Ro had to go in to the office."

An arch look. "*After* you stopped by his place to check and see if they needed anything."

I tried for a casual shrug, had the feeling I'd failed miserably. I didn't know what had taken me to his house (the address of which I had because I was Maddie and I'd needed it for all those interactions with lawyers and judges and the paperwork that had followed). But I didn't know why I'd stopped and parked instead of driving by, like I'd intended. Didn't know what had brought me to the door, what had made me knock not once but *three* times.

Only that I had this feeling I couldn't ignore.

And it had propelled me into Ro's life.

Or *kept* me in it, rather.

"I hadn't seen his new house yet," I tried, not buying that myself, even though that was a small part of it. Yes, I'd come home to visit in the years since my move, but Ro had been in Australia dealing with custody things, so I hadn't seen it.

Or *him*.

A man who...well, *fine*. A man who I wouldn't mind ending my dry streak with, a man who I might be slightly obsessed with —*had* been slightly obsessed with—for years.

"And Jack?" Mel asked.

I cocked my head. "What do you mean?"

Another arch look. "You two came in like peas in a pod, laughing and talking the entire way."

I shrugged. "He taught me how to kick a soccer ball."

"Ah."

"What?" I asked, seeing Mel's mouth curve up.

"The kid is sports crazy," she said. "It's the way to his heart."

"Along with food," I countered, "Mrs. Cinnamon Swirl Cake." Grinning when her cheeks went a little pink. "Something he talked nonstop about on the way here."

Another thing to bond over.

Food was also one of my favorite things—cinnamon swirl cake especially. Which Mel knew. Because she grinned and shrugged good-naturedly. "I had to find a way to tempt you home to meet this little one."

It hadn't taken much tempting, honestly.

It was time for me to come back, to find another project.

To find something else to fill my life.

"Well, hopefully," I said, pushing that thought away, "I'll be able to enjoy your baking prowess more often now that things have settled and the office is established."

Mel smoothed her hand over the baby's head. "Hmm."

"What?" I didn't like the look that entered Mel's face, didn't like her tone.

It said she saw too much.

"Nothing," Mel said softly. "Just know that I'll be happy with how ever much time—and yourself—you feel comfortable giving me."

How ever much time *and* myself.

My stomach convulsed, bile burning the back of my throat, but before I could deflect—or cut and run like my instincts were screaming at me to do (Too close! Too fucking close!)—Mel squeezed my shoulder and stood up. "How about that slice of cinnamon swirl cake now, huh?"

———

"Maddie?"

I blinked, jarred from my thoughts, and glanced in the rearview. "Yeah, bud?" I asked softly.

It was getting late, the sun having set not long before.

Mel and Ash had offered to keep Jack overnight, but he'd mentioned wanting to play some online game with friends, and, as set up as Mel and Ash were for their own kids, they didn't have the right type of computer for the tower defense game Jack wanted to play.

So, I was driving him home and would stay with him until Ro got back.

Which, based on the small amount of his conversation I'd over-heard, would be much later.

He had problems.

But—I mentally shrugged—I could fix them.

"Do you like my dad?"

My fingers tightened on the steering wheel, but luckily, I didn't drive us off the road, more of that *Too close! Too fucking close!* feeling swirling in my stomach.

I *had* always liked Ro. He was smart and kind and funny and... it had to be said, the hottest man I'd ever met. I respected the fact that he lived his life the way he wanted, and respected him even more so when he dropped everything and changed all of that to bring Jack here.

To support his kid.

To be present in his life even though things were—obviously—not going smoothly.

"I like your dad a lot, honey."

Silence, long enough that I glanced in the rearview again, debating with myself. Jack was a sweet, funny kid and it had taken him all of a couple of minutes to warm up to me. Part of that was because I knew his favorite YouTuber and that Roblox was an online game (even if I didn't know what a tower defense game was). Part was him remembering me from FaceTime with Ash and Mel and that he'd taught me how to properly kick a soccer ball.

The rest was...I was good with kids.

I liked them and I figured they genuinely understood that. But...I also thought that part of it was because my life had left me understanding exactly how precious innocence was.

And how much it hurt to lose it.

Which was why I gave Jack a little slice of me.

"I was like you," I said softly. "I lost both of my parents, so I know what it's like to feel alone." Another glance in the mirror, seeing his gaze was still pointed out the window. "And your dad lost his dad so we *both* know how important family is." A breath. "But more than that, I know what it's like to have to make a big move away from everything I know."

"What do you mean?"

Pain rippled through me, but I was determined to help Rome smooth things over. "When my parents died, I moved here to California. It was hard and I missed my friends and I felt lonely, especially when my grandpa and grandma didn't seem to want me."

More quiet, then, "My grandma wants me," Jack said softly. "She told me I'm her best helper."

"I bet you are." Because despite the tension between him and Ro, he was a good kid.

Just hurt and left behind and sad.

"And your aunts and uncles love having you here," I added.

"I changed Evie's diaper."

"You did?" I asked, genuinely surprised.

"Yup."

"That was really nice of you."

"It was no big deal"—I heard the shrug in his tone—"even though Uncle Ash always complains about how bad it smells."

My lips tipped up. "It really isn't." Though I was betting it was just a pee one, based on how casual Jack was about said smell. "But it is a big deal that you helped."

He fell quiet again and I debated saying more, wondered how receptive he would be, especially given that we'd known each other for all of a day. A wave on the phone while I was FaceTiming with Mel or Ash didn't count. It wasn't like we'd sat down and chatted for hours.

But that we were having this conversation at all told me that he trusted me, at least a little bit.

So, I decided to just...say it.

"You know, your dad probably feels sad that he missed out on so much with you. Stinky diapers and all," I added lightly.

Silence from the back seat.

"And I know it probably doesn't feel like it now, but you *are* really lucky to have a guy like him as your dad. He's a good person and loves you very much."

More silence from the back seat.

But he wasn't looking out the window anymore.

He was staring up at me.

Our eyes met in the rearview.

I waited and when he didn't reply and I had to look back out at the road, I gave him the out. "So, what's the point of a tower defense game, anyway?"

# FIVE

Ro

Christ, I was fucking tired.

But, as usual, I had Maddie to thank for fixing my problems.

International custody battle? *Cool, no big deal. I got you, boo.*

Potential illegal conduct that might implode my company? *Here's a contact who can help you smooth things over before it's too late.*

Making sure my kid was fed and in bed and supervised? *That's the easiest task yet. Watch me bond with him like you haven't been able to in—oh—the entire year you've had him.*

"Fucking superpowers," I muttered, just glad she was using them for my good.

Maddie was a woman who could take over the world given the right opportunity.

Thankfully, she was on my side.

Why that was, I didn't know, but I suspected it was because she was close to Ash and Ash would be upset if my life imploded. Which would then affect *her* life and—

"Maybe she's just a nice person, asshole," I said under my breath, pulling my car into the garage and hitting the button to close the door behind me.

Yeah, she was.

And I was too tired to think further on the subject. I needed to go in, thank her, let her get back to her own life, and then hopefully get some sleep.

Because my brain was spinning and I needed some fucking rest.

Sighing, I got out of my car, headed for the door that led inside, and moved quietly through the house. The kitchen smelled fucking great—way better than after any time I'd ever made anything in it. Spicy with undertones of sweet and—

My eyes caught on a sticky note on the counter and I paused, reading the words on the small square of paper.

*There's a plate for you in the fridge.*
*And chocolate cake.*

*-M*

*I know it's not cinnamon swirl but it's the best that I can manage in a pinch...plus, Mel won't share her recipe with me. She says it's the only way to bribe me home.*

I grinned, feeling strangely light after the shitshow I'd been dealing with over the last hours.

Chocolate cake and a homemade meal. Yeah, that wasn't a bad thing to come home to.

I moved to the fridge, snagged the covered plates, and set them on the counter before going in search of Maddie.

But when I moved into the living room it was to find her laid out on the couch, the TV playing softly in the background, her lips parted and her breathing slow and steady.

Jet lag? Or Jack tiring her out?

Or some combination of both?

Backing up quietly, I turned away, the action strangely difficult for some reason, and moved quietly to the stairs.

Jack's door was cracked and I nudged it a little wider, poked my head in through the opening. My son was sprawled out on his bed, body half uncovered, legs and arms akimbo. I crept in through the mess of clothes and toys, stuffed animals that spoke of the seven-year-old little boy he still was and the gaming gear that foreshadowed the tween that wasn't all that far away, and I felt the loss of him all over again.

I'd missed out on so much.

And...he hated me.

Smothering a sigh, I tugged the blanket up and over him, flicked on his nightlight, and then tiptoed back out of his room. Pausing, I hit the switch to kill the overhead lights, shut the door, and moved back downstairs.

Food in the microwave.

Chocolate cake in my belly.

Then eating the delicious dinner Maddie had left me.

And *then*, I was out of time.

I needed to decide if I was going to either leave her to sleep on the couch, move her to the guest room and risk waking her, or gently guide her out of sleep, make sure she was awake enough to drive, and send her packing.

The last, I might have done a few years ago.

Kick 'em out before they get too close.

But this was Maddie—a woman who'd gone to bat for me and won over my kid and made me chocolate cake and dinner and—

Yeah, there was no way I was leaving her to wake up with a stiff neck and sore back.

She was going to sleep in the guest room.

Decision made, I did the dishes then went down the hall and made sure the room was ready for her—sheets on the bed, toilet paper in the bathroom, overhead lights off but bedside lamp on, blankets pulled back.

Then I returned to the living room, staring down at her like a creeper, feeling my heart squeeze tight because she was a force of nature when she was awake, but right now, sleeping quietly, her breaths soft puffs glazing the air, she seemed fragile, breakable.

*Beautiful.*

Her lashes had been settled on the tops of her cheeks, but now they fluttered.

I stilled, waited for them to open, for her to catch me being a creep, but they didn't do more than slit open then closed again, lashes resting back onto her skin.

Dreaming, I realized.

Her exhale was a little louder this time, almost a word, but I couldn't make it out.

Didn't matter anyway.

I needed to get her to the guest room and me to bed.

I bent, carefully slid my arms beneath her, started to straighten—

"Ra—mmm," she moaned softly.

Freezing, I held my breath.

Her legs shifted on the couch, hips moving on the arm I'd slipped between her and the cushions.

"Row—mmm," she moaned again.

And this time when I froze, it was with my heart pounding.

Because that sounded a lot like my name, and she was rubbing against my arm and—

"Rome."

That *was* my name, and it was a moan, and her hips were moving restlessly, her neck arching, head digging back into the pillows.

"Rome, oh God. *Rome.*"

I had to admit, my dick had twitched at the first hint of my name on her lips, a twitch that turned into a bit of chub at the actual soft rasp of it leaving her tongue. But this—the breathy moan, the gyrating hips, the way her head pressed back into the pillow—and I'd gone hard.

Fully erect and pressing against my zipper.

"Fuck," I whispered.

Her eyes opened.

Not just a little bit this time.

But fully, her blue eyes staying unfocused for several long moments before they cleared. "Rome?" she whispered.

"Yeah, baby," I said. Or maybe rasped. Or maybe—

"Is this a dream?" she asked softly.

I shook my head. "No, it's not a dream."

Her eyes went a little wider, tongue darting out to taste her bottom lip. How had I never noticed they were so pink and plump before? How they reminded me of other things that would be pink and plump and...*slick.*

Her breath caught and my gaze slid from her mouth, up to hers, seeing that the remnants of sleep were well and truly gone...

And *heat* was in its place.

Her hips shifted again, rubbing against my arm, making my dick twitch. "It's *not* a dream?" she asked.

Desire and amusement in the same moment. That shouldn't be possible. "Not a dream, baby."

"Oh." She swallowed.

Once.

Twice.

I opened my mouth to offer up the guest room and a full night's sleep, to offer up the fact that I could cook her breakfast in the morning.

But I didn't get the words out.

"*Oh*," she said again. Her eyes flicked down. "It's not a dream and you're—"

That tongue flicked out as her gaze slid toward my groin, where—yup—my hard ass dick was making its presence very known, pressing against my zipper and since I was bent over her, preparing to lift her...it was pretty much right in her face.

Smooth.

Real fucking *smooth*.

I cleared my throat, slid my arms out from beneath her. "Sorry, baby, it's been a bit of a dry streak with Jack and all, and I—"

"Why are you apologizing?"

Because my hard dick was in her face.

*That* was why.

"Maddie—"

She sat up so quickly that we nearly bonked heads. "Don't apologize."

"I—"

But I didn't finish the statement.

Because then her mouth was on mine.

# Six

MADDIE

Part of me was still convinced I was dreaming, that Ro couldn't be turned on.

Not from me.

Not this close to me.

But the rest of my body and mind was very aware of this being real, and it wasn't because of the muscular arms that were wrapped around me, or the heat of him on my skin, or even the spicy male scent in my nose.

It was the rough groan vibrating through his chest and into my own.

*That* was something I'd never be able to imagine.

*Before* anyway.

Now it was committed to memory, same as the way his body had stilled before his arms around me tightened and his lips parted and...he kissed me back.

Rome Hutchins was kissing me.

With tongue.

In a way that immediately swept me out of the vestiges of sleep and straight into reality.

And how fucking glorious the real world could be.

His arms flexing and drawing me closer against a strong chest, while at the same time he moved, shifting me back so I was pressed against the couch cushions. Pinned to them by his big body moving over mine. All while his tongue tangled with mine, not tentative and uncertain, but big and brash and so totally Rome.

He kissed like he lived his life—wild and free and intense.

I hoped he fucked like it too.

Because I really needed an orgasm.

I grinned when he broke away, giving us both a heartbeat to breathe, but that didn't last long because then he was kissing me again, but this time with *hands.* They'd moved out from behind me, one bracing himself by my head, taking some of his weight, but not too much, which I was grateful for, needing that feeling of a heavy, male body pressing into me. The other slid over my sensitized flesh, teasing me through the layers of my clothes, beginning at my shoulder, drifting down along my side, cupping my ass through my pants, coasting to the back of my thigh, and—

I moaned.

Oh, *that* was nice.

Hitching my leg around his waist, angling our hips so that our pelvises aligned.

Hell *fucking* yes.

He was big and hard and had us perfectly aligned.

One movement and his dick was pressed to my clit.

Yeah, there were a lot of layers in between, but it still felt good...and it boded well for my future orgasms that he could both kiss so well and line up our bodies with just one smooth motion.

Now, if we could only get our clothes off then things would be fucking perfect.

"Baby." He leaned more heavily into me and I found that my eyes had slid closed. Opening them, I saw his chest moving rapidly, his deep brown eyes molten pools of dark chocolate, and the slightest bit of indecision entering his expression.

Right.

No.

I didn't want indecision because he thought I might not be with him. I didn't want to stop because he was worried this was too much too fast, too much out of the blue. Things I knew had to be in his mind because he was a good guy and he might live wild and free—or *had*, anyway—but he was that *good guy*.

He'd slow things down.

Send me off in my car to my own house—or hotel room, anyway.

That wasn't what I wanted.

Not with him pressed into me and his kiss what it had been and that sleek movement that had perfectly lined up our pelvises.

"*Baby,*" he said again, a little more firmly this time, hand sliding back up, fingers weaving into the strands of my hair.

"Rome," I whispered, arching so that our hips ground together, so that I rocked against the hard ridge of his erection.

He grunted, pushed against me.

Oh.

That was nice. *Really* nice.

My clit was a happy, happy girl.

I lifted my hand, threaded my fingers through his hair and drew his mouth back down to mine.

This kiss was hotter—somehow—than before, his tongue showing no mercy as it drew mine into battle with his.

And that was what this felt like.

A battle. A war. A fight to the death.

And then...

A conquest.

And how good it felt for the man to conquer *me*.

He started by knocking my hand free and kissing me deeper, until I felt like I was drowning in him, but just when a blip of panic began to enter my mind (because I needed to breathe some-time this next century), he released my lips. His hand had stayed in my hair, though, and now it tightened, tilting my head back as his dropped, mouth finding my jaw, kissing along it to my earlobe, gently laving it with his tongue—

"*Oh!*" I gasped, shuddering when his teeth bit into my skin.

The small hurt was soothed just as quickly, his tongue darting out, lips teasing me before he trailed them down my throat, nibbling at my collarbone.

At the same time, he moved his other hand from by my head and down to my waist, finding the edge of my shirt and dipping his hand beneath, stroking it across my stomach.

I shivered, arched to give him better access.

And then his mouth was on mine again.

His hand didn't stop, thankfully. It kept moving over my stomach, back and forth, back and forth. Hot, rough, and teasing.

Still touching me, still kissing me, but I felt the slender threads of control enter his body, knew that this was all he would give me.

And that was driving me slowly insane.

So...I decided to take him along with me.

One final battle that would drive us to the end, that would decide the victor, that would take us both into oblivion.

And, Christ, but I had to stop with the war analogies.

But my mind had latched onto them, and I couldn't—

His fingers trailed over my middle, teasing along the waistband of my pants but not beneath them, like I wanted, not slipping into my underwear and stroking through my wet pussy. And not moving up and cupping my breasts, rolling my nipples either.

Just back and forth.

Back and forth.

Back—

I made my move.

Snaking a hand between us, I cupped him firmly.

He jerked, groan rumbling through him, and I took advantage, finding the edge of his T-shirt, yanking it up. The material bunched between us, but—thank fuck—I'd managed to draw it up enough to expose his gorgeous brown skin, flat abs, and a set of pecs that told me he must love a barbell and chest press.

"Sweet Jesus, that should be illegal," I muttered, sliding down, losing the lovely connection of our hips, but getting my mouth on his skin, that strongly muscled torso, wiggling further when he groaned, when he let me kiss him and touch him and—

I made it down, dislodging cushions and smooshing my body against the arm of the couch.

But I managed to reach the final battlefield.

The button on his jeans.

I flicked it open, located the tab of his zipper, started to tug it down, exposing the head of his cock—hard, thick, precum glistening at the tip.

"Maddie—"

I leaned in, dragged my tongue over the hot, silken skin, the salty tang hitting my tastebuds—

"*Oh!*"

Hands slid under my armpits and dragged me back up.

It only took a fraction of a second.

But I lost the war.

# SEVEN

RO

S wollen lips.
  Mussed hair.
  A lush body moving on mine, hands on my skin, knowing I should stop this but unable to push Maddie away in this moment.

Not when it had been too long.

Not when it felt too good.

She worked at the waistband of my jeans, opening the button, tugging down the zipper.

I should stop this, let us both get to bed, think about why, all of a sudden, I was here making out with Maddie, getting hard for her, a moment away from saying fuck it all—

And fucking *her*.

A tongue flicking out and lapping at the head of my cock.

I moved without thinking, reaching down from where she'd somehow wriggled her body between us, hooking her beneath her armpits and dragging her up.

That dangerous tongue made another appearance, slipping out, sliding along her bottom lip, making my cock harden further.

I ignored it, wove my hand back into the silk that was masquerading as her hair.

"What the fuck do you think you're doing?" I growled.

She hitched her leg over my hip, grinding against me. Her hand, that sneaking fucking hand, moved along the side of my body, shoved between us, fingers grazing my skin, heading south again. "I'm trying to make us *both* happy," she murmured, tilting her chin up, leaning close, and dragging her lips along my jaw, nibbling lightly. "I'm in desperate need of an orgasm." A beat, her fingers twitched. "And I think you are too."

Then her fingers wrapped fully around my cock.

And I remembered that, yes, I was in desperate need of an orgasm too.

And...

Fuck it.

Fuck *her*.

I inhaled, reached between us to capture her hand, but I didn't peel it off my cock, just held it there. "You sure, baby?" I asked softly.

Her blue eyes darkened to navy, lips parting, the hot puff of her exhale glazing my mouth. "Yeah, Ro," she murmured. "I'm sure that I want you to fuck me right now."

And that was when I stopped thinking, worrying, needing to check in with her, needing to process what had changed between us and just...

Decided to give us both those much needed orgasms.

Reaching down, I snagged the edge of her shirt, drew it up and over her head, tossing it to the side and freezing.

Grinning.

"Christ, baby," I muttered, appreciating the view for a second before reaching behind her and unclasping her bra, dragging it down her arms, completing my thought. "You've got to have the most gorgeous tits I've ever seen."

Hot in a shirt.

Sexy as fuck in just a bra.

And like this? Naked, the hard pink buds of her nipples on display for me, calling for my lips, my teeth, my tongue? Totally control shattering.

I bent and did what I needed to do, kissing the soft globes, sucking at the taut buds.

Learning what made her gasp and moan and arch against me.

Doing it again and *again* until her hips were grinding against mine, until her hand had squirreled between us again and was on my cock and stroking, distracting me, taking me closer to the edge of control, making my vision close in.

Tasting her.

Teasing her.

Teasing *me*.

I released her breasts, began kissing my way down her belly, making short work of the leggings that covered her lower body, that encased those lush thighs and ass, the muscular calves, the cute feet, and—more important to the part of my mind that was functioning at the moment—that glistening cunt.

"Rome," she whispered when I tugged off her underwear and tossed it somewhere to the side. "I don't need you to—" Her eyes flicked down toward the apex of her thighs.

I spread them wide.

Yeah, she didn't.

I hadn't even touched her there yet and I could see she was soaked.

My mouth watered.

So, no, she didn't *need* me to get my mouth on that pussy, to warm her up, to use my lips and tongue to drive her crazy. She was ready. I could thrust in deep and fuck us both into oblivion.

But I didn't work that way.

"No, baby," I murmured, nipping at the inside of her thigh when she shivered, tried to inch them closed. "You don't *need* me to lick you until you come on my mouth"—I glanced up, ran my tongue up through the center of that sopping pussy, her shiver and soft moan enough to have me doing it again, and *again*—"but I'm going to anyway."

And then I did.

Sucking hard on her clit, pinning her hips in place when she bucked, learning her body like it was my fucking job.

Listening to her moans come faster, feeling her body shiver, her legs close around me.

And then listening to her come.

Shattering on my mouth, hands in my hair, pulling at the strands so hard that I worried I'd be bald, but then I didn't care because I realized she was tugging me up and over her, yanking at my shirt.

I reared back and tossed it to the side while she reached behind her, grabbed her purse, and...

Pulled out a condom.

Probably I should demure, stop this before we both did something we would both regret.

But desire was a pulsing drum in my veins, making my hands shake as I took the condom and tore it open. She was shaking just as violently, as though the orgasm she'd just had hadn't assuaged her need at all, had only fueled it.

I managed to get the condom down and then her purse was on the floor and she was laying back, legs bending, the sides of her knees coming to my waist.

Instinctual.

Perfect.

Like she was made for me.

But before that thought could penetrate, could send me off into a fucking panic, her legs twitched around my waist and she ordered, "Orgasms."

That had my mouth curving, my body bending, mouth sealing over hers, the tip of my cock notching at her entrance.

I pushed in, feeling the tight sheath of her, the heat, tasting her moan on my tongue, giving my own back. She shifted, allowing me to seat myself further, until I was bumping up against the edge of her womb, until I was all the way inside, until our bodies were perfectly aligned.

"Move, baby," she murmured, breaking the kiss, head pressing back against the cushions.

I obliged, pulling out, thrusting in, nowhere near in control, nowhere near gentle.

But she was right there with me, meeting me stroke for stroke, hips grinding, nails digging into my skin.

"That's it," she moaned, eyes flashing open, holding mine. "That's it. Right—"

Her pussy convulsed around mine, a vice that razored through me, splicing the filaments of thought, sending me pounding into her once, twice, *three* more times.

Then my orgasm was on me.

Barreling through me.

*Destroying* me...with pleasure.

I collapsed, barely managing to not crush her, to catch myself, but not to catch my fucking breath.

I was panting like a racehorse.

But eventually I managed to suck in some air, return back to Earth, and gently shifted off her, my dick still hard and nowhere near done with her. But I had a kid now and—I looked up, relieved when the lights were still off, when there was no sign of Jack—we'd managed to do this without scarring him half to death.

I needed to get both of us dressed—partially anyway—and to the bedroom.

Where I could continue with her order of *orgasms.*

But, first, I had to take care of the condom.

With that thought, I pushed off her, sliding out of her, liking the soft protest that formed on her lips, wanting to be back in her pussy just as much as she so clearly wanted me inside.

"Be right back," I told her.

I grabbed my pants from the floor, stepped into them and wrestled my still-hard dick into them before walking down the hall and into the bathroom.

All of a minute later, the condom was off, my hands were washed and I was heading back to the living room.

To Maddie.

Trying to pretend that thought didn't do something to my heart.

Only when I got there, my heart didn't react. My gut did.

Like it had been punched.

Maddie wasn't where I left her, lax and heavy-lidded on the couch.

She was dressed, complete with her shoes on and her purse slung over her shoulder, tugging her hair back into a ponytail.

I stopped dead.

She merely finished with her hair then glanced up at me, smiling wide, moving over to me, her tone light when she said, "Thanks for the orgasms."

She rose on tiptoe, pressed a kiss to my cheek. Then dropped back down while I processed that blow...and why the fuck it *was* a blow when I wasn't looking for anything serious, anything more than a long overdue getting-off session.

"See you around, Ro."

A hitch of her purse.

A spin on her heel.

And she was gone, the front door latching quietly behind her.

# Eight

## Maddie

"This is killing you, isn't it?" Ash asked, leaning back in his desk chair and plunking his feet onto his desk.

*That* was killing me—his germ-ridden shoes on his desk—not the rest of what he was insinuating.

"No, it's not bothering me at all." I told him, even though his shoes were the last thing on a long list of things that were bothering me, most of them starting with Ro.

The rest of them *ending* with Ro.

And his long, thick cock.

And his big, strong body.

And his rasping groan when he'd come inside me.

And—

Ash laughed. "Liar. This office isn't in Maddie shape and that's killing you."

I blinked, forced myself to get that night a couple of days ago out of my brain—never mind that I'd been dreaming of Ro kissing me ever since then.

Well, okay, it *began* with the kiss. And ended...with that big, hard cock.

"Jax is great at her job," I forced out, trying my best to stop thinking about Ro's dick.

Dickmatized.

It was a thing.

And anyway, Jax *was* excellent as Ash's assistant. Something I knew without a doubt because I had trained her extensively, had spent hours on the phone with her over the last years, and then had turned her loose to soar off on her own Post-It laden wings.

Would I have prepared for this very important meeting this way?

No, definitely not.

But Jax had her own system, and I wasn't going to judge—not to Ash, anyway.

In the comfort of my own hotel bed? Absolutely, I would be breaking down each and every mistake that I'd flagged.

Because it wasn't done *my* way, and my way was clearly the best.

*Clearly.*

"Yeah," Ash said. "Jax is really good at her job." A smile my way. "Because you made that happen."

I shrugged, as though it was no big deal—even though it wasn't in the least. Ash had trusted me, promoted me, welcomed me into his life and family. I knew exactly how valuable that was to have, and it was why I would do anything for him and his family.

And Rome.

My pussy clenched, remembering exactly what he'd done for me.

Glorious.

The burning stretch as he'd pushed inside, the aching internal muscles that had lasted until this morning, when I'd woken up without feeling the soreness, the physical memory of him.

And part of me had mourned.

The rest of me had daydreamed. Then I'd dug into my suitcase and pulled out my vibrator...and maybe I was sore right now for the same reason—minus the side of one Rome Hutchins.

"I just did what anyone would do," I began, even though Ash was already shooting me a bemused smile and shaking his head.

"Don't even try it, Maddie," he said before I could go on with prevaricating. "Not everyone would do even *one* percent of what you've done. And even more impressive, you do it because you're a good person who doesn't care if you get anything in return. Now," he went on, tone going businesslike, probably sensing the panic welling up in me, knowing that he was treading too close to everything I preferred to keep buried. "What are your plans now that everything is settled in Europe? Do you want to come back and work out of this office? I know Mel would prefer it." He slanted me a look. "And maybe Jack would too."

"I—"

"We're expanding offices here and would like to open up a distribution center in Nebraska—to shorten our shipping times to the East Coast—so that could be a great project for you to head. That's only a three-hour flight and you could still headquarter here."

"I—"

"Oh!" He tapped a finger to his chin. "Roger's leaving, and he needs a replacement. I know you want to get more into the finance side of the company"—Roger was the current CFO—"and if that still interests you, there would be time for you two to work together." He leaned forward, started jotting down notes. "I can loop him in on a meeting with us all together."

"I—"

He glanced up, finally seeming to realize that I wasn't an active participant in this conversation. "Or we could find you something else if none of that excites you."

Nebraska in the winter didn't sound fun.

Starting a new construction project, staffing it, putting in place a management system and guiding the whole process from start to finish did.

Immensely.

But—

"What?" he asked softly, putting down the pen and leaning back in his chair. "What is it?"

*I fucked your brother and it was fantastic!*

Something that wasn't the least bit part of this conversation, even though that intrusive thought was right there on the tip of my tongue, encouraging me to self-destruct.

Luckily, I was good at tamping those thoughts down.

I *wasn't* good at this conversation.

"I..." was all I got out before I ran out of steam.

Ash got up, rounded the desk, genuine concern on his face, and that sliced through me. Because I didn't want to ruin what I had, didn't want to lose him, to lose them all, and this...might make them all hate me.

"Maddie," he murmured, crouching in front of me and taking my hand.

"Brooks offered me a job."

He rocked back slightly, fingers convulsing around mine. "And what did you say?" he asked gently.

"I said..." I pressed my lips together, released them, and exhaled. "Yes."

———

Later that afternoon, after the meeting with Ash's business partners had gone smoothly, albeit not as smoothly as it could have if *I* had put it together, I was hiding in my temporary office and trying to pretend that Ash wasn't mad at me.

I'd seen the flicker of hurt on his face, knew my leaving him was seen as a betrayal.

Even if he'd slapped on a smile and congratulated me, had told me I would be great at Brooks's company.

I felt sick.

I'd waffled for too fucking long before considering the offer, knew what risk it would bring.

But also, it was a great opportunity and—

And maybe I was getting too comfortable with the Hutchinses, too reliant on them.

Maybe I needed to have a backup plan now that Europe was done and life was moving in new directions.

Who knew how long it would be before they got sick of my shit and wanted me to move on?

This just...gave me a parachute before I jumped out of that proverbial plane.

Simple, right?

I huffed out a laugh.

Sure. Whatever.

*Super* simple.

Sighing, I closed my laptop, decided that I might as well pack up and head back to the hotel. I could do emails from bed with a fluffy robe and a side of room service.

Only, after I'd hitched my bag over my shoulder and walked out of the office, I spied Rome pounding up the stairs, face thunderous and strides long and fierce—

Oh boy.

I wanted that long and fierce and—

Panic rippled through me.

Oh *God*. I couldn't see him. Not after he'd fucked me on the couch, and all of my dreams, and my time with my vibrator that morning, and...my thighs all but quivering with him still fifty feet away.

I swallowed hard, yanked at the nearest door handle in the long line of offices, and all but tumbled into one of the rooms.

Thankfully, it was empty.

"Ro!" I heard Ash call, a heartbeat after I'd shut the door almost all the way, leaving just a tiny crack.

For emergency purposes.

Like blatantly eavesdropping.

I was doing it for the greater good. One hundred percent.

"Hey," Ro said, voice all sharp edges.

"What's up?" Ash asked, tone immediately concerned as I was.

"Jack and I can't make dinner tonight."

"Why not?" Ash asked. "We can move it later if he has practice or something—"

"No," Ro growled and sighed. "Sorry." Another sigh. "He got in trouble at school and refused to apologize. I told him he can't go to soccer until he does...and he told me he hates me." A beat. "Again."

My stomach twisted.

"Shit, bro, I'm sorry—"

Ro sighed again. "It's not your fault. It's just..." His voice dropped, making it so that I had to practically press myself to the wooden panel in order to hear him. "He hates me, and that's not going to change when I keep taking things away that he loves. But I can't let this one go. He can hate me, but he needs to be able to function in his classroom and make friends and...not be an asshole. So, I'll take him hating me as long as it's going to help him be a better person."

Ash said something in response, but I couldn't hear it well and couldn't tell if that was from the pounding of my pulse in my ears or the fact that they'd moved away from the door.

It didn't really matter.

Because I'd heard enough.

*I'll take him hating me as long as it's going to help him be a better person.*

Yeah, no.

That didn't work for me.

Ro was a good guy.

Jack was a good kid.

I was going to fix it.

It was time to get down to eliminating this bad business.

# NINE

Ro

"One time," Jack's teacher was saying the next week, this being the second of as many meetings I'd had to drop everything to come to school and attend in as many weeks, "we could write off as a warning and work to make sure it doesn't happen again, but twice"—she winced and shook her head —"I'm sorry to say that I need to bring the principal in and we'll have to put together a behavior plan."

A behavior plan.

For my kid.

For my *seven-year-old* kid.

Christ, I'd failed at a lot of things in my life, but hearing Jack's teacher discuss the details of this fucking *behavior plan* and I'd never felt more like a failure.

Not. Fucking. *Ever.*

"I know he's been through a lot in his short years," the teacher said, smiling sadly and reaching across the table to squeeze my hand. "This isn't a comment on him or your parenting. This is just a way to get him the help he needs."

"He sees a therapist," I felt like I needed to point out.

I wasn't a total fuck-up. I knew that Jack needed a safe space to unpack, and yeah, maybe it was ego talking or maybe it was that I'd been kicked a few too many times in the junk lately, but I needed the teacher to know that I was doing my best to help my son with *all* aspects of his life.

The trouble was...I was failing.

Because I couldn't bring his mom back

And I couldn't leave him in Australia.

Not only because Jack's family there was wholly unsuitable, but because Jack loved my mom and my siblings and he needed the stability they could provide.

And, well, *I* needed my kid here.

Even if I was a total fuck-up who Jack hated.

"That's really good, Rome. He needs that."

Which were the words I thought I needed to hear, and also... they were words that didn't make one fucking bit of difference.

Silence fell for a moment, and I found myself struggling to find something to say to break the awkward beat, but what did one say in a parent meeting like this that I hadn't already said?

Luckily, his teacher had my back.

"I'll speak with the principal and then reach out to you with available dates."

I nodded, stood when she did, extending my hand and shaking hers. "Thanks for your time."

"Anytime."

We exchanged goodbyes, and then I walked out of the class-room, thinking about failures and the upcoming meeting with the fucking principal and...

I sighed.

My son.

Who was sitting on a bench in the courtyard between the class-room, arms crossed and chin resting against his chest.

Not pouting exactly, but not far off.

Full-on sullen teenager at seven.

I sent a wish and a prayer that Jack's shitty attitude now meant I would get off easier during his teenage years.

Though, knowing my luck...

Unlikely.

I walked across the shaded space, sat down on the bench next to him.

And waited for my son to say something.

But he didn't react except to cross his arms more tightly and scowl.

Smothering a sigh, I asked, "Do you want to talk about it?"

An immediate, "No."

Now I was smothering another sigh, but I didn't push further. This wasn't the time or place. Snagging his backpack in one hand, I stood up from the bench. "All right," I said evenly. "Then let's go."

I'd gotten the call from school in the middle of a meeting— something I would now need to take later tonight after Jack's homework was done and we'd both eaten dinner.

Alone. No Hutchinses alongside us.

Just me and my son eating food I would have to cook. Food that wasn't Mel's chicken and dumplings.

I'd dropped everything and come to school because it was my *kid*, but I wasn't looking forward to cooking and sure as shit wasn't happy about missing Mel's homemade meal that would be a hundred times better than whatever I whipped up.

I also wasn't looking forward to passing along the news of his bad behavior to Ash, explaining why we were skipping out on family time.

"Can I have a snack before I go to soccer?" Jack asking, coming up beside me.

My pace faltered, but only for a second because Jack kept walking and we were almost at the car, and I didn't want to have the subsequent conversation on the sidewalk in front of school in case things blew up between us.

And they were likely to blow up.

Which was why I didn't answer as I bleeped the locks, waited for Jack to get in, closing the door behind him before tossing his backpack in the trunk and getting into the driver's seat. I jabbed at the button to turn on the ignition, put the car into drive, and took off out of the parking lot.

Only then did I say, "You can have a snack. But you know that you're not going to soccer tonight—"

"What?!"

"And you need to call and talk to Greg"—his coach—"and explain exactly why you won't be there tonight or at the game on Saturday—"

"*What?!*"

Luckily, the locks on my car engaged automatically.

Otherwise, I think Jack might have tucked and rolled.

As it was, I blew out a silent breath. "We had this discussion last week, bud, and you know Greg will back me up. Getting into a fight at school?" I checked traffic, turned the corner. "One was bad enough. Two? That's not going to fly with him." A beat. "Or me."

"That's not fair."

"Sometimes life isn't fair." I shrugged. "But the best thing you can do is try to stop making things so hard on yourself."

Jack didn't fight me on this—we'd lived together long enough that I figured he knew by now that when I set a firm boundary that boundary was held. Instead, he fell silent and stared out the window. The waves of his anger were still palpable from the driver's seat though.

I'd just turned into our driveway when he deigned to speak again.

"I hate—"

"Me," I finished for him with a tired exhale, hitting the button to open the garage door and pulling the car inside. "Yeah, I know, kid. You hate me."

I turned off the car, popped open the driver's side door.

"You still have to do your homework, though."

Same as I had to get on a call and reschedule that interrupted meeting, and...

I hit the button to close the garage, moved into the house.

Same as I had to figure out what the fuck I was going to cook for dinner.

# TEN

"No!" Mel groaned, throwing her cards down with a huff and sitting back in her seat. She jabbed a finger my direction. "You're a freaking shark."

I grinned, calmly began sorting the cards into their respective decks, Ash, Mel's twin, Tiff, and her husband, Wyatt (who was Rome and Ash's brother) helping as well. "There are no niceties excepted while we play *Nerts*."

A card game that combined solitaire and speed with the object being to get rid of our decks as quickly as possible.

Also something we were all extremely competitive about.

There were no holds barred.

"You blocked me from putting down my two," Mel grumbled.

I bumped her shoulder, began sorting the stack of cards in front of her—see? I was a nice winner—and said lightly, "You wanted me back in town."

A pout. "Not to kick my butt in my favorite game."

Ash leaned over and kissed her temple, smiling in a gentle way that mirrored what I was feeling in my belly. Warm, squishy, and so much fucking respect for this woman who had overcome so much. She'd been assaulted and reduced to a shell of herself, and she'd fought back, becoming someone I admired so intensely it almost hurt just being in the beautiful glow of her.

I loved that she was confident and comfortable enough to argue with me.

"She beat you fair and square, sweets," Ash murmured.

Mel huffed. "I just had a baby." But her lips were curved up, and she reached behind her to grab the glass of wine—the one glass she allowed herself since she was breastfeeding. A small sip before she grinned over at me. "Rude."

I was on glass...three? Four?

Either way, I was feeling really good—*really* good after my victory at *Nerts*, muahaha!—and just grinned back at her, asking, "Rematch?"

Her glass was plunked back onto the table, her fingers laced and hands stretched. "You bet your bottom, we're having a rematch."

The kids were asleep—minus Jack who was at the other game table.

The wine was out and everyone was partaking—minus Jack, who had a glass filled with sparkling cider.

The games were getting heated—*Nerts* (my favorite) at the table I was sitting at and *Ticket to Ride* at the other with everyone else.

Yup. There were now *two* tables at game night.

The Hutchinses were a big family to begin with—six brothers, Jeremy, Wyatt, Asher, Eli, Ro, and Rowan, and one sister, Cora, along with an adopted brother, Rafe. Eight of the originals, and then adding in the significant others and their kids, and chaos reigned.

Hell, it was lucky we weren't at three tables.

When the kids got old enough to all be interested in playing, I supposed there would be at least that many.

Still, it was a good night.

This was one of the things I'd missed the most over my years on another continent. Not kicking butt in *Nerts*, but feeling like I was part of this family, even if just for a few hours, even if just on the periphery, even if just in the tiny corner I'd carved out for myself.

Game night equaled the *best* night.

I...well, until I'd met Ash and been invited along, I'd never had anything like it.

Which was why I passed Mel's sorted—and shuffled deck—back to her, set up my own cards, and then said, "Go!"

We all flew into action.

Cards were thrown, others were blocked, some were tossed back with a rebuff or a narrow-eyed warning about cheating.

(Which usually garnered an unrepentant shrug and continued game play).

And eventually, victory was found.

Not by me, alas.

But by...

Ash.

"You are so totally sleeping on the couch tonight," Mel said, her nose wrinkled and lips set to full pout. But her eyes were dancing with humor. And Ash clearly didn't take the threat seriously, my boss leaning over to kiss her long enough to eliminate any sign of amusement or frustration, leaving her quiet and soft when he straightened, ran the backs of his knuckles over her cheek. "Want a cookie, sweets?"

Mel smiled. "That *I* made?"

He nodded, mouth curving. "Maybe."

A pat to his cheek. "Then two please."

I had to look away from the scene, not because I was uncomfortable—shows of affection were common in the Hutchins crew—but because the scene I'd just witnessed was so sweet it hurt.

Like I had a cavity.

Or had eaten an entire tray of Oreos and felt suddenly sick.

"How about I get you both some?" I asked, hopping up from the table.

"You don't have—" Mel began.

But I was already heading into the kitchen, avoiding further exposure to the scene like I'd successfully avoided being alone with Ro since Orgasms two weeks before.

Because I was implementing plan *Fix It*.

Because that took time and energy and wasn't an easy fix.

Because it was safer to avoid him.

All of my efforts at evading ended, though, with one ill-timed escape from a sweet scene at the card table.

Rome was standing in the kitchen, beer in hand, bottle tilted up as he drank, and—

Fuck, it was a miracle I didn't faint on the spot.

His throat worked as he swallowed, the long column of the strong neck that I'd kissed and nibbled at on full display. The cuff of his T-shirt was stretched around his lifted arm, reminding me of how powerful his body was. His pecs, his back. His...I swallowed when my gaze drifted down his torso enough to see the hem of his tee riding up, exposing a strip of flat abs and the waistband of his boxer briefs that was just peeking out above his jeans.

Hot. As. Fuck.

My pussy clenched, and maybe I made a sound, or maybe he just felt that I was watching him like a freaking Peeping Tom.

Either way, he stopped drinking, lowered the bottle, and—

His eyes hit mine.

Heat.

Need.

My thighs trembled and my stomach rolled over and my heart began pounding faster. Moisture gathered between my thighs.

*Clunk.*

He set the bottle on the counter, leaned back, elbows wide as he gripped the edge of the granite in those big hands. I'd frozen about two feet into the kitchen, struck still by the gorgeousness of him, and he took the opportunity to study me, gaze sliding down slowly and then back up.

Returning to mine for a long moment.

I watched the words bloom on his face, saw them coming, but I could have never expected what would actually come off his tongue.

"I wanted to see that look on your face all night long, baby."

Roughened velvet sliding over my skin, drifting up my thighs, feathered between them.

"Wh-what?"

He pushed off the counter, prowling toward me.

Closing the distance.

Ten feet.

Five.

*One.*

"You left," he said, finger sliding softly over my jaw.

"You had Jack, and it was late and—"

"I had plans to break in the mattress in my bedroom."

Heating flooding through me so rapidly, my knees nearly buckled. "I-I—" I paused, the words processing. "I—you haven't...?"

"No, baby, I hadn't fucked a woman in my bed." His mouth twitched. "*Still* haven't."

He hadn't slept with a woman in his bed since he'd *moved in?* That had been years now. Only...that wasn't what sent my pulse pounding even more rapidly through my veins. It was that he'd wanted *me* to be the one to break it in.

Me.

That didn't make sense.

"I—"

His palm flattened on the side of my neck. "We had that moment, and you left before I could make sure you were okay."

My heart squeezed, hard, at the same time my pulse settled.

*Before I could make sure you were okay.*

The chivalry of the Hutchins brothers.

It was less about me, less about *me* in that bed, and more about...

Making sure a woman he respected—me, for the record—was good.

That tracked. That made sense.

That...cooled the desire threading through my insides.

The doorbell rang, and I distantly heard someone call, "I'll get it!"

Orgasms and a fun night. Looking after someone he'd shared his body with. A kindness from a good man.

And, seriously, *of course,* Ro wouldn't think I was anything more than—

"What are you thinking?"

I glanced up—not realizing my eyes and focus had drifted—and saw that his face had clouded, darkened with thunderstorms.

"Nothing," I said quickly.

His hand on my throat twitched. "Bullshit, baby. Tell me what the fuck it was that brought that look to your face."

My lungs froze, heated desire and frosty panic running up and down my spine, warring.

Unnerving.

"I—"

"Rome," a voice said.

His gaze shot over my shoulder. "Not now."

"No." It was Ash speaking, I realized, my boss's tone penetrating and immediately sending worry coursing through me. "You need to come right now."

Ro was stiff and statue still. I could practically feel his control splintering as the urge to snap at his brother welled up inside him.

But then he exhaled, the rage faded. He dropped his hand, and stalked from the room.

I sucked in a breath, shoved down feelings, shored up others, and turned.

Ash was there, expression stark, eyes seeing too much.

But he didn't comment, just followed me when I walked from the kitchen and moved to the front door.

Which was open.

A figure standing on the threshold.

I frowned, not understanding what I was seeing at first.

Not until I heard Jack's voice.

"Mom!" he shouted, sprinting forward and throwing himself into the woman's arms.

# ELEVEN

RO

Watching and feeling my son shove past me and throw himself into Carrie's arms fucking hurt.

I couldn't lie.

It *eviscerated.*

But more importantly, I was tucking away the pain of that sight and doing my best to focus.

Because *Carrie* was standing on my brother's porch...looking thinner than I'd seen her last and without the sun-kissed glow on her olive skin.

But very much alive.

And currently crouched, her arms wrapped tightly around Jack, her face buried into his neck, her shoulders shaking.

Crying.

Reuniting with our son.

Reuniting when she was supposed to be dead.

"What the fuck?" I whispered. "What the actual fuck?" I didn't know if it was rage that I was feeling or fear or relief or—

I was going to be sick.

Going to throw up right there in the entryway of my brother's house and—

A hand suddenly found mine, and I jumped, glanced down, and saw that Maddie had woven our fingers together. She held on firmly, body coming up next to mine, shoulder pressed to my side.

As though she were going to brace me, keep me from collapsing.

As if she had a chance of keeping me upright if I went down.

I'd crush her.

And...just that train of thought settled me, snapped me out of my shock, made it so that I could focus.

"Is that—?" Ash moved to stand by my side.

"Yeah, that's Carrie," I managed to force out from between my numb lips.

"I—" Ash blew out a breath. "What the actual fuck? Did she rise from the goddamned crypt?"

Suddenly, I felt like laughing and this situation wasn't the least bit amusing.

Because it had been four years since I'd fought for custody. Eight since she'd left in the middle of the night without a word, leaving me wondering where in the fuck I had gone wrong, what I'd done to ruin things, and leaving without telling me she was pregnant.

Because...I had Jack's birth certificate and I'd done the math.

She'd known she was pregnant when she left me.

And thought I—

Pain pulsed through my center, a dagger slicing up and into my heart.

Because she must have thought that I wouldn't be a good husband, a good...dad.

I guessed based on the shitshow that had been Jack and I coexisting over this last year, she was probably right.

I inhaled sharply as that thought stabbed at me again.

Maddie's fingers tightened and she leaned more heavily against me. "Breathe," she whispered. "It'll be okay." Her voice dropped even more, until it was barely audible, until I had to strain to hear it. "I'll make sure it is. I promise."

I jolted, but before I could really process that, really sit in the heavy truth she'd laid on me with that assurance, with her confidence that she'd work her Maddie Magic and make this okay—and that I believed that at a bone-deep level—Carrie lifted her head from Jack's neck and grabbed his shoulders. "Get your stuff, baby. We're getting out of here and going home."

My jolt this time was stronger.

My "What the fuck?" louder.

"Seriously," Ash muttered.

But it was Maddie who reacted first, squeezing and then releasing my hand. She moved to the door and gently touched the back of Jack's head, getting his attention. "Hey, bud. Can you go grab a cookie from the kitchen?"

Jack, I realized now, was unnerved, his eyes wide and skin pale. Shock setting in or confusion. No. There was worry there, worry that...what?

I exhaled, moved forward when he seemed to waver. "It's okay, bud," I murmured. "Your mom isn't going anywhere"—I narrowed my eyes at Carrie, warning her—"and I bet she'd like to try a cookie too."

Jack's shoulders lifted and fell on a breath, but for fucking once, he didn't argue with me, just tried to take a step back.

Carrie's hands tightened.

I saw it happen, saw her nails dig into my son's shoulders.

He winced.

"*Carrie.*"

Her head jerked, gaze coming to mine.

It was slightly unfocused, slightly unhinged, slightly...crazed.

*Fuck.*

But thankfully, me snapping out her name had her hands opening, and Jack was able to step back. He took another—this one in the direction of the kitchen—but then he paused, teeth nibbling at his bottom lip, glancing between me and Carrie, indecision on his face.

"No one's leaving, bud," I said softly. "Promise."

Carrie straightened next to me. "We're—"

"*I promise,*" I repeated, holding his eyes.

Jack held them right back. For long enough that Carrie rocked forward, started speaking again. "Jack and I are going—"

I shifted to the side, standing in front of her. "No one's going anywhere right now, okay?"

My son wavered again.

Then he nodded.

And turned for the kitchen, Ash trailing after him. Maddie stayed right where she was, a couple of feet back from Carrie...and blocking the rest of the doorway, I realized.

A physical barrier between the woman who I'd once hoped to marry...and the son I loved, but who hated me.

Christ.

So not the fucking time to think about that.

There were way more important things to focus on—

Starting with the fact that Carrie wasn't dead. And standing on Ash and Mel's porch. And—

*She wasn't fucking dead.*

"Why don't we talk on the porch?" Maddie said softly, her gaze going between me and Carrie. "We can sit down at the table, eat a cookie, figure out where we are."

The air tightened, and Carrie looked from me to Maddie for the first time.

Her expression darkened, eyes flashing. "And who the fuck are you?"

"Carrie," I warned.

Maddie's chin came up, and she stepped a little closer to Carrie. "I'm the person who can either be your best ally or your biggest fucking enemy," she said in a voice like steel. "So, you can take a breath, wipe your fucking face, and sit on the back porch eating delicious fucking cookies while figuring out where we are and where we're going. You can keep it together so you don't worry your son any further, or you can make the wrong decision and continue to fuck with your life and your kid and—"

A muscle in Carrie's jaw twitched, and I saw it before the words came out of her mouth.

That she'd lost the hold on her temper.

Fuck.

"Car—"

Carrie stepped forward, closing the distance between her and Maddie and doing it in a quick movement. "I repeat," she snapped. "Who *the fuck* are you?"

Maddie, Magical Fucking Maddie, held her ground, shoulders ramrod straight, chin raised. "I'm—"

"I don't care," Carrie hissed. "Now get the fuck out of my face and *give me my goddamned son!*"

Maddie moved this time.

But it was because Carrie had lifted her hands and shoved Maddie. *Hard.*

I shot forward, managing to snag Maddie's arm and drawing her to a halt before she hit the floor. A tug had her back on her feet, but that was all the movement I could spare. Because, after the push, Carrie had started toward the kitchen.

And that wasn't fucking happening.

Neither was screaming in Ash and Mel's house, and screaming when Jack was around, when other kids were sleeping and might wake up and get scared.

I caught Carrie by the arm, drew her back to the door and onto the porch.

Away from Jack, from the other kids.

Maddie followed, closing the door behind herself.

Of course she did—the following *and* the closing of the door.

Looking out for everyone around her.

"Carrie," I muttered, moving down the wrap-around porch. "Get a fucking handle on it. Jack is just inside and you're screaming."

"I'm screaming because I went home and my son was gone!" She yanked at her arm and I released her. "I'm screaming because my baby wasn't there!"

"Yeah," I said, crossing my arms. "That doesn't feel good, does it?"

Which was the absolute wrong thing to say.

Because if I'd thought that Carrie had lost her temper before, she proved me wrong.

Because my question made all hell break loose.

# TWELVE

MADDIE

I sighed and quietly closed the door to Jack's bedroom, padding out into the hallway and hating that I'd just sat with a little boy who'd been hiding his tears as I'd read from a popular book about wizards and witches and bad, *bad* guys.

He'd tried to hide the tears.

Same as he'd tried to hide the fact that he was upset when the cops had been called and had to physically restrain Carrie, as he'd tried to hide that he saw the scratches on his father's face.

The cookies he'd retrieved had gone uneaten.

Then again, I hadn't much felt like eating, myself, after the scene at Ash's house.

Babies and toddlers crying. Me having to make a call to the police. Rome pushing Carrie back and taking my arm, drawing me back to the front door, *through* the front door.

Which was when he'd earned those scratches.

Something that stood out in sharp relief as I approached his office and peered through the open door. He was on the phone, head hanging, listening with his cell pressed to his ear, a series of "Uh-huhs" the only glimpse to this side of the conversation.

I moved into the room, rounded the desk, and propped a hip against the surface, blatantly listening to Rome as he paused with the *Uh-huhs* and started talking.

To his lawyer, apparently.

Certainly, the smartest call he could make.

Because this entire situation was a mess, something out of a teledrama, something that was so fucking wild I could hardly believe it.

Carrie back from the dead.

The. Dead.

And, yes, I was fully aware it wasn't actually *the dead*.

Because if she had been dead, she wouldn't be here now and—

Regardless, it was still dramatic and unbelievable and...why the fuck couldn't she have kept it together long enough for us to understand where the fuck she'd been?

At the very least, Jack deserved an explanation.

And Ro, too, considering all they'd both been through over the last few years.

*Why did they leave me?*

I closed my eyes, clenching the edge of the desk, remembering. I had asked that question over and over again, not getting an answer that made sense, that satisfied.

Because there wasn't one.

Not in a world where people stayed dead, stayed gone.

Except...that wasn't Jack's reality now, was it?

And I honestly didn't know if he had it better or worse with Carrie back. He'd been healing, inching forward. Troubled, for sure. Struggling with Rome. But finding a place in the Hutchins clan, surrounded by family that would love him unconditionally.

And now his mom was back.

But...it was after she'd left him.

Would there ever be a good enough reason to justify that?

I was hard pressed to think of one.

"Yeah, Todd," Ro muttered. "I'll write everything down, film what I can, and I'll get the videos from my brother and send them over."

More *uh-huhs*.

More pauses and listening.

"Right. Thanks," he said after a few more minutes. "Talk to you soon. Uh-huh. Yeah. Bye." He hung up, sent his phone clattering to his desk, and sighed. "Christ," he muttered. "This isn't seriously my life, is it?"

I, unfortunately, couldn't disagree with that, so I settled for scooting a little closer, ignoring the pulse of heat when our legs tangled, and touched his jaw, bringing his focus from his lap up to my eyes. "It'll be okay," I murmured.

He exhaled, lids sliding closed. "How is it going to be okay?"

I didn't have an answer for that—or not anything other than telling him, "We'll work it out. Promise."

Now his head tilted back, leaning against the top of his leather chair, eyes opening again. "And when you make a promise, you keep it."

That had my heart thudding hard once against my rib cage.

Because *I'd* said that.

Long ago. When I'd been in Europe and we'd been in the weeds of the custody battle, when it had seemed hopeless that Ro would ever get his son here.

*I'd* said that.

And we'd gotten Jack here.

"Yeah," I whispered, hand sliding from his jaw to his shoulder, kneading the taut muscles there. "Promises are meant to be kept."

Silence fell then, and it was pained, tense, nearly as tense as his trapezoids.

Which I kept kneading, working out knot after knot after *knot*.

Until he groaned and shifted forward, arms going around my

middle, head dropping against my collarbone. "What the fuck am I going to do, baby?"

"Keep talking with your lawyer. Give him what he asks for. Use our connections as needed. And speak with Jack's therapist to make sure you're giving him what he needs."

His arms convulsed. "You make it sound easy."

I laughed. "I don't think anything about this is going to be easy. But you and Jack both have me and your family and we're all going to sort this shit out, yeah?"

Arms still around me, head still on my collarbone, he nodded, and, hold tightening further, he said, "Because you're *the person who can either be your best ally or your biggest fucking enemy?*"

I winced.

I didn't like a scene, especially in front of a kid who was great and had been through too fucking much, but that was perhaps a bit dramatic.

And it hadn't diffused anything.

"I'm sorry," I said, guilt heavy in my belly. "I inserted myself somewhere I shouldn't have"—clearly, a major fault of mine— "And I saw she was on edge. I shouldn't have said it and I am really sorry—"

His head flew up, brows furrowing. "What the fuck are you talking about, baby?"

"I—" My throat worked, swallowing hard, heat hitting my cheeks...and hitting lower.

Because his face was right there.

Because his lips were *right there.*

Because his eyes were...warm.

Oh shit. Oh shit. *Oh shit.*

"Or maybe I need to make this clearer." He fixed me with a look. "What the fuck are you *apologizing for*, baby?"

I swallowed again, that heat inside me swelling up, making it hard to think, to speak. "For overstepping my bounds," I managed to whisper.

He stilled and I found myself freezing, worry knotting my insides, sending me even closer to the edge of panic.

His eyes, though, they were still warm.

Then his head dropped back and I lost the warmth, the gorgeous brown irises with their golden flecks and—

He laughed.

Loud and long and it was the best sound ever.

He sat back, and although I'd lost the warmth of his eyes (though I'd gained the warmth of his laughter), I didn't lose the closeness.

This was because his hands had dropped to my waist and he'd hauled me off the desk as he'd moved, drawing me toward him, plunking me into his lap. And suddenly a *lot* of things were a lot closer—his squeezable pecs and strong arms, that tasty column of his throat, his abs and thick thighs, and...something else that was thick and growing hard beneath my bottom.

Something that had heat blossoming in my middle, heat traveling down, spreading between my thighs. Moisture gathered, my pussy clenched, and my stomach fluttered.

Butterflies.

The man had given me butterflies with one simple movement.

One hand slid up along my side, up, up, *up* until it cupped my jaw and he was tilting my face toward his.

"Baby?" he asked silkily.

"Yeah?"

And seriously, why was my voice all raspy?

Probably because my head was spinning and my pussy was aching and I was having a really hard time focusing.

"Why have you been avoiding me?"

# Thirteen

Ro

She froze for a long moment. Then blurted, "We should talk more about Carrie."

I saw the panic in her eyes, so I knew that for the diversion tactic that was.

"No," I said, drawing her closer—which had the pleasurable side effect of dragging her over the hardening length of my erection. "We shouldn't."

The scene had been fucked.

The cops had been called.

My lawyer had a plan.

There were a shit-ton of questions that needed to be answered and a fuck-ton more preparations that needed to be made as a result of the woman I'd asked to marry me and then had disappeared in the middle of the night pregnant with my kid and then had died and *then*...hadn't, I supposed, showing up at Ash's front door.

But that wouldn't be solved, not tonight.

And Jack was asleep, I assumed, since Maddie had been glued

to my son's side from the moment we'd come back, and I knew she wouldn't leave him, upset and alone unless he was fully out.

Because Maddie was a good person.

Because she cared about Jack and me and my family, and had done it fiercely for as long as I could remember.

So, even though I was fucking rattled and upset and worried, part of me believed her.

That it would all be okay.

It would be a shitty, fucked-up rollercoaster along the way, because of course it would be. But it would be *okay*.

And we'd already boarded the rollercoaster, rising, clicking along on the track as we ascended.

The rest of the ride was unknown.

All we could do was hold on.

How it would all pan out, a fucking mystery.

But not one that was going to be solved tonight.

Something that *could* be solved, however, was why the hell the woman whose lush ass was currently in my lap had fucked my brains out, had given me an orgasm that had been freaking glorious—something that had nothing to do with the long-ass pussy hiatus I'd been under—and then had disappeared.

Seeing Jack at Ash and Mel's and not here.

Conveniently busy or on a call or out of the office.

Sitting at a different fucking table at Game Night.

"Why have you been avoiding me, baby?" I asked again.

Stiff. Still. Frozen.

She started to push off my chest.

Yeah, that wasn't happening.

I tightened my hold on her hips. "Why, baby?"

Another push.

I held her fast, waited.

"I've been busy with work."

Tilting my head to the side, I studied her face. That almost sounded right. *Almost*.

I leaned in so that our breaths mingled, held her eyes. "Liar."

She sucked in a breath, body still again, hands on my chest, mouth a millimeter away. "I'm not lying. It's always insane in the office and then I've been—" She clamped her lips together and I watched the subterfuge come to life on her face.

What the fuck?

My fingers tightened further, digging into those sexy hips of hers.

I wanted to hold on to them while I fucked her from behind, while she sat on my cock and rode me hard and fast.

"What have you been doing, baby?" I pressed.

"Noth—"

"Maddie, baby, I know you've got connections and Maddie Magic and are good at solving problems, but I think we've gotten to know each other pretty well, so, *think*, baby. I've got this in my mind—to get an answer to the question I asked." I slid one palm over, running it along the strip of skin that had been exposed by her position, trailing it over silken flesh bared above the waistband of her jeans. "Have I ever been one to let it go?"

I said that.

But at the same time, I remembered that there *had* been a time when I'd let it go.

When Carrie had left.

But I didn't want to think about Carrie. Fuck, I didn't want to think about her.

"No," Maddie said. "You don't like to let things go."

So, in reply, I just lifted an eyebrow.

She sighed, but I knew I'd won when she settled more heavily against me. "I *have* been working"—she narrowed her eyes at me—"but I've also been working on...you."

My other eyebrow joined the first. "What?"

Pink on her cheeks. "Well, you and Jack," she whispered. "I've been trying to figure out how to bring you guys together."

That felt like a fist had wrapped around my heart and squeezed. Hard. "*Baby*," I rasped.

"It's nothing."

It wasn't nothing. It was fucking *everything*. It was what I'd been moving toward for four years in my mind, inching toward even though I hadn't realized how completely it was written on my soul until this moment.

This woman was for me.

"What did you do?" I rasped.

That pink flared, and I drew her even closer, sliding my hand up her back, threading my fingers into her hair, holding her in place when she tried to look away. "Nothing, really," she said. "Not so far," she added quickly, probably in response to my expression. "I just put out some feelers and...um..." Her eyes slanted to the side.

"What?"

"I kind of called in a favor and to get you and Jack field-level seats." She swallowed. "I figured it would be a good place for you and Jack to bond."

That was amazing. So...why did she still look guilty?

"Maddie," I warned.

She winced. "Well, I kind of coerced Bonnie into helping me make it seem like it would be your idea and connections that got the ticket."

That explained the lunch meeting on my calendar tomorrow with my business partner, Augustin, who had season tickets to the local professional soccer team.

"Jesus," I muttered. "You're devious."

Now she paled. "I know I overstepped. I just—"

"You just?" I asked when she didn't go on.

She shook her head, eyes not on mine.

"You care," I said. "And it's part of what makes you so fucking wonderful, baby."

Her nostrils flared on a sharp inhale, gaze coming back to mine.

And I gave into the urge that had been eating at me, using my hand in her hair to draw our mouths together.

Fucking *explosion.*

Desire flaming through me, my body acting on instinct as I stood from the chair, plunking her on my desk. Shit on top clattered and fell off, and my chair shot back, hitting the wall. But I didn't give a fuck. Not when I was ripping her T-shirt up and over her head, sending her bra flying. Not when I was guiding her back so she was spread out on the desktop, and I was reaching for the button on her jeans, yanking them off her legs, taking her underwear with them.

One jerk and her ass was perched on the edge.

I parted her legs, put that pretty cunt on display.

"Ro," she gasped.

I knelt, drew her forward, and...

"*Fuck,*" I groaned against her pussy, as the taste of her hit my tongue, sweet and a little tart, but all woman.

All *Maddie.*

Tongue working, I slid a finger into the wet clasp of her pussy, felt it clamp around me. I wanted to feel that on my cock.

But I wanted to make her come first.

So...I did.

Sliding another finger in, sucking at her clit, using my free hand to draw her more firmly against my mouth while I worked her pussy. No mercy. Not stopping until she was writhing, head restless on my desk, sending papers and pens onto the carpet. Not stopping until my name was tumbling off her lips and she tightened around my fingers and—

"*Oh God,*" she groaned. "Oh, my fucking God."

She was still coming, still convulsing around my fingers, but I couldn't wait any longer to feel that around my cock. I pulled out and stood, unbuttoning my pants while I yanked out my wallet, retrieved a condom.

Pants down. Cock out. Condom on.

Maddie up on her feet and flipped, front pressed to the desk, that gorgeous ass in the air.

And then *I* was groaning as I stroked inside her slick heat, feeling her clamp around me.

"*Fuck,*" I growled, thrusting hard and fast, probably *too* hard and fast. But she'd propped herself up onto her elbows, was looking at me over her shoulder. Her hair was a fucking mess, her eyes half mast, her lips swollen. But the best was the glimpse I got was of the side of her tit, watching it bounce each time I pushed into her.

The view sent me close to the edge.

Too fucking close.

But she was right there with me, head dropping back, eyes sliding closed, hips arching and meeting each of my strokes.

Faster. Harder.

"Rome!"

*There.*

I came apart, barely a second, barely a heartbeat after her, my orgasm so violent it nearly sent me to my knees as wave after wave of pleasure burned through me.

"Fuck," I murmured a minute, a century, however the fuck long it took for me to return to my body and regain my ability to speak.

It wasn't Shakespeare, but it got my point across.

The half of her mouth I could see tipped up. "Yeah. Exactly."

I forced myself to slide out, but instead of leaving the room this time to take care of the condom, I scooped her up, carried her to the attached en suite and plunked her on the counter. Then I did the necessary business, narrowing my eyes as I buttoned up my pants, took off my tee and tugged it over her head. "Stay," I ordered as I went and retrieved her clothes.

She *stayed,* and when I returned, I scooped her back up, carried her upstairs to my bed.

"Ro," she whispered after I pulled back the covers and tucked her beneath them. "What are you—?"

I climbed in after her, hit the switch for the lights, and tugged her back against me.

"Tired," I muttered, not wanting to have an argument, not exactly knowing what to do with the fact that I knew she was mine.

"I—" She cut herself off on a sigh. "Right," she whispered. "You're tired and it's been a long day and you need—" Another pause before she sighed again. "You should go to sleep, honey."

Yeah.

I needed that.

And she did too, which was why I just pressed a kiss to her nape, tugged her closer, and let my lids slide closed.

Holding her, sleep came fast and heavily, the events of the day rolling over me in a wave that stole any hope of staying awake.

I was *out.*

With Maddie in my arms.

Only, when I woke...

She was gone.

# Fourteen

MADDIE

"So, I told her," my words coming a mile a minute as they were wont to do, especially when one of my plans came to fruition, "to arrange a meeting between Rome and Augustin"—one of Ro's business partners who happened to have season tickets to the local professional soccer team—"and I figured it would come up naturally."

Plus, Augustin had a company that ran compliance for a lot of the big companies in the area.

I knew that he could help Rome with business *and* with a stubborn little kiddo.

Who was great.

But stubborn.

And who was wounded after his fucking mom had shown up out of the blue.

Gritting my teeth, I clenched my fork tighter and scooped up a bite. "Their businesses align and it would be a you-scratch-my-back, I'll-scratch-yours kind of thing."

"Right," Mel said, daintily taking a bite of her sandwich.

I smiled, even though I wasn't sure how natural it was, considering it felt like my lips had been encased in drying clay. Stiff, dry...breakable.

Probably because I was exhausted after lying awake in Ro's arms for hours the night before, listening to the soft, even sound of him breathing, ensconced in his heated strength, wrapped in the spicy scent of him. Pussy aching, limbs lax, shivers from the orgasms—yup, that was with an *s*, as in plural, as in orgasm*s*, as in I hadn't thought a man could do it once, let alone twice, but clearly, Rome Hutchins wasn't like normal people. At all.

But even more than my body and clit, and it had to be repeated, my pussy, which had been used and abused and pleasured in the best possible way, I'd laid in silence next to him...

And tried not to panic.

This wasn't me.

I didn't sleep with men—well, I *slept* with men in the sense that both of us got off. But I didn't cuddle in their beds with their arms around me and their soft breath in my ears. I didn't lay there wishing I could let it be more than mutual pleasure and exchanged orgasms.

I lay there thinking that Ro was better than any of my past lovers.

That he was better than my vibrator—and I'd invested in an incredibly good, expensive one that had every bell and whistle possible.

And it didn't make me come nearly as hard as Ro fucking me fast and furiously against his desk had.

I shivered.

"I have a question for you."

I blinked, realized I'd been in Sexy Time Land, and glanced up from my salad, from my cup of coffee, from my pastry—because one couldn't be at Molly's Bakery and *not* have a pastry—and met Mel's eyes.

We were grabbing lunch because Ash had taken the kids to an indoor play place.

Something that had happened because I'd spoken to Jax about Mel seeming a little overwhelmed and had her schedule a few sections of time during the week for Ash to get some one-on-one time with both kiddos—something *else* I'd noticed him missing since he'd returned to work.

Win-win.

Mel got a break. Ash got time with the kiddos when they were happy and not overtired during that evening witching hour.

And I got a little time with my bestie.

"Shoot," I told her, lips curving.

"You make it all look so easy."

My brows shot up. "Make what look so easy?"

Mel tilted her head to the side, shining brown hair swinging behind her. "Managing people, solving problems, jumping into a new job—"

I winced, knew with the soft chiding comment that Ash had shared about Brooks offering me a job, that I'd—deep breath—taken it. She wouldn't give me a hard time about *not* sharing—she was too sweet and gentle and *nice* to do that. Hell, she would cheer me on from the sidelines, knowing it was a great opportunity for me.

But, all the same, I felt that soft admonishment deeply.

"You make it seem effortless," Mel murmured, "but I know it's not easy."

It wasn't.

I sometimes felt pulled in so many directions looking after Mel and Ash, Ro and Jack, and the rest of the Hutchins crew who had sewn their ways into my heart, that I was going to be ripped to shreds.

I just...did it anyway.

Because I hadn't had that and I craved that and maybe some small part of me worried that if I actually focused on myself, actually let myself have a moment that just belonged to me, they would wake up one day and not want me—

"Work is far from easy," I said, shoving that thought away. "But you know me, I love working on new projects and challenges."

"Hmm."

I picked up my pastry—one of Molly's famous chocolate croissants—and took a huge bite, the layers crumbling as I bit into it, making a huge mess on my plate and the table and—it had to be said—on my lap. My eating was a diversionary tactic, but it was one that had delicious consequences...namely that buttery taste, the light, crunchy texture, the bite of dark chocolate on my tongue.

"I'm happy when I'm busy and I love solving problems," I said, once I'd chewed and swallowed, relieved my tone was as light as my words. "You know I'm at my best when I'm juggling ten plates at once."

Mel tilted her head again. "And all of them full of everyone else's issues to fix."

I let my mouth curve up. "Well, yeah."

Because it was easier to fix everyone else...and not myself.

She shook her head, sighed softly. "Ash is going to miss having you in the office, you know?"

I was going to miss him.

But it was time.

Before he moved on and found out he needed something—some*one*—different.

"I've been out of the office for four years, Mellie."

My friend smiled and shook her head, as though she saw straight through my bullshit. In fairness, she probably did. "Except, you guys talk a half-dozen times a day."

I winced.

Ash and I *did* do that.

And it probably wasn't all that conducive for a relationship between a man and his wife and two kids.

"I'll call less—"

"Maddie." Mel reached over, took my hand. "That's not what I'm saying. I'm happy to hear from you, happy Ash has you at his back. That Rome does, too." Her expression turned knowing. "Because one of those plates you love juggling has been filled with his stuff for years now, honey."

I inhaled.

"Which is what I was going to ask." Mel squeezed lightly then released me, leaning back and picking up her own croissant. "Why are you so invested in Rome?" A beat that seemed to speak volumes and certainly had me launched right back into my panic-filled fog of being in Ro's bed only hours before. But then she set her croissant down, added gently, "And Jack."

My exhale was too sharp, relief at the out she'd given me nearly burning my lungs. "Jack is an innocent kid who's been through too much."

That, right there, was enough of the truth.

It wasn't the *whole* truth.

But it was enough.

"You know I lost my parents," I murmured. It was more complicated than that and deeper and heavier and...it didn't matter. That was the past. Jack was living it now. "You know it was tough feeling like I didn't have a place," I said. "It's important to me that Jack has a different life."

Not as an outsider.

Not feeling unloved.

Not thinking that he wasn't enough.

"Are you sure that's *all* of it?"

"Well, now that Carrie's back, that's become a lot more complicated," I said, going for diversion again.

A diversion that worked, thankfully.

Because Mel's expression changed and the words started tumbling out. "Oh my God!" she exclaimed. "Ash and I were talking about that. How the heck..."

We spent the next forty-five minutes trying to figure out how a woman could have left her kid, and what we were doing to protect Ro and Jack—and the other kids from another dramatic scene. I filled her in on the little I knew, made sure that Ash had sent the security footage from the cameras on their front porch over so Rome could forward it to his lawyer. But there were more questions than answers, and then our conversation shifted to the babies and her job as a book cover designer and—

Anything but me.

Because we didn't need to focus on me.

Because...if I didn't solve everyone's problems, didn't make everything perfect, didn't fix it all then they would look at me and find me lacking and—

Then they would tell me to go.

# FIFTEEN

Ro

"I'm not so sure this is a good idea," I muttered to Blake, my attorney, and we headed down the hall and toward the front door.

Because the bell had just rung.

And it was, presumably, Carrie.

Who I'd spoken to on a conference call with my attorney that morning.

She'd seemed...much more like herself. Without that edge in her tone, no sign of the unhinged woman she'd been a few days before.

Just...Carrie.

And now she knew where I lived.

That didn't exactly make me feel good, but Ash and Mel had Jack, and my attorney and I were trying to see if we could have a calm, relaxed meeting to straighten some things out.

Some things being where the fuck the mother of my child had been for the last four years.

And why the fuck everyone had thought she was dead.

"Things are complicated when it comes to family law"—Blake slanted me a look—"as you well know, but judges appreciate when parties try to come to a consensus on their own before bringing their drama to the courtroom."

That made sense.

Pretty much the only thing about this entire situation that did.

Blake clapped me on the shoulder. "I'll be here the entire time, I promise. And if things go really bad, my boss said to call her."

Rebecca Darden.

Pitbull of an attorney, and one of the connections that Maddie had given me. Rebecca—or Bec as she preferred—had been too busy to do more than consult on my case, but she'd referred me to Blake, who'd, ultimately, been a huge part of the reason that Jack was here in the States now.

So, even though I didn't like the idea of Carrie being here after the shit she'd pulled—hell, the scratches were still healing on my cheek—I trusted Blake.

And his ability to get Bec Darden involved as necessary.

"Ready?" he asked, reaching for the handle.

"To face my not-dead ex who wants to take my kid away?"

Blake snorted. "Not going to happen."

I exhaled. "Right." I wasn't going to lose Jack. I just...I didn't know how I would *keep* him.

Because I'd never had him in the first place.

Because...he hated me.

There was a knock—quiet, almost timid, as though the person on the other side didn't want to disturb me. Or didn't want to repeat their actions from Ash's house.

Christ.

I sighed, braced, then looked to Blake.

"Good?" he asked.

I nodded.

He opened the door.

And the bottom fell out of my world.

Hours later, head pounding, mind totally fucked, I got in my car to take a drive.

There was an observatory nearby, a quiet parking lot I could pull into, could sit on the hood of my car and stare out at the glimmering lights below.

A slice of peace when things were falling apart.

And what Carrie had told me that evening...I wasn't sure how I could keep them together.

I sighed, shook my head. I could barely begin to process all she disclosed, or how much the subsequent lawyer fees were going to cost me as we figured out a custody agreement.

Because that was where we were heading.

And maybe that was why I didn't head to my parking lot beside the quiet observatory, didn't sit on the hood of my car, looking out at the rolling hills and twinkling lights and the huge messy demonstration of life below.

Instead, I headed to my brother's offices.

He wasn't there.

He was home with his wife and his kids...and with Jack, who was camped out in the room he'd stayed in so often that it had become his.

But Maddie would be.

I don't know how I knew.

I just...*did.*

And after I'd driven across town, the silence inside my car almost too noisy, almost pressing in on me, almost *suffocating*, I knew that the reason I went to Ash's offices instead of the observatory was because there was only one person inside them that could help me breathe freely again.

I turned into the lot, lungs immediately loosening when I saw the rental car that Maddie had been using parked close to the building beneath one of the bright lights that illuminated the space.

I slid into the spot next to it, turned off the engine and sat for just a second with my head against the steering wheel.

Then I exhaled.

"Okay," I whispered and straightened, getting out of my car, moving toward the glass front doors. I reached for the handle, tugged—

It was locked.

*Shit.*

Leaning in, I peered in through the glass, finding the lobby empty—not a surprise, considering it was late. Maddie's office was on the second floor, though, and—

The security guard, Tim, came around the corner.

Thank fuck.

I waved as he approached.

"Hey," he said, pushing the door open. "Ash isn't here—"

"I know," I told him. "I was looking for Maddie."

Tim's face changed, and I didn't like the blip of want that entered the other man's eyes. Fucker. She was *mine.* I wanted to stand over her, claim her as mine, snarl at anyone who'd dared approach. A terrifying prospect considering that the last time I'd been with a woman I'd wanted to make mine she'd...well, that woman had been Carrie.

Fucking nightmare.

But to Tim's credit, he just pushed the door a little wider, nodded toward the staircase. "She's upstairs, working as usual."

Right. *As usual.*

"Thanks," I muttered, taking the stairs two at a time and moving down the hall to Maddie's office.

I could hear her voice before I even made it halfway, confident and a little musical, and instantly, I felt something come alive in me. Or maybe, it settled, soothed—

Or maybe, I didn't give a fuck.

Because I was striding into her office.

She immediately sensed I was there, looking up with the phone pinned between her shoulder and ear, her fingers resting on her keyboard. For one second, that beautiful mouth dropped open in surprise. But then she recovered. Because of course she did.

"I'll call you back."

And she didn't even wait a second before she hung up the phone, before she was out of her chair and moving toward me, rounding her desk, not stopping until she reached me in the doorway. "What's the matter?"

"My lawyer suggested Carrie and I get together with him for a meeting."

Her eyes went wide. "What?"

"We did that earlier tonight."

"*What?*"

"I—" My throat was dry, the words stoppered up. "Fuck, Maddie. This is such a goddamned mess."

"Is Jack okay?"

My heart clenched hard. That was her first question. Christ, this woman was fucking amazing.

"He's okay."

A relieved breath and she nodded then reached by me and closed the door before stepping back, taking my wrist and drawing me toward one of the chairs in front of her desk, pushing me down into it.

But when she went to sit in the chair next to me, I found I couldn't let her, found that I needed her close, her body against mine, so I snagged her wrist and drew her down onto my lap. And Maddie, of course, allowed me to have that, didn't fight me, didn't argue.

Just settled in my lap, cupped my jaw, and softly ordered, "Tell me everything."

# Sixteen

I'd demanded he tell me everything.

But I couldn't have predicted the next words he said.

"Carrie was in a coma."

I blinked.

"She went on vacation." He shook his head. "It was supposed to be just for a couple weeks, but she got in an accident when she was there. Somehow her ID was lost and they couldn't identify her and—" He shoved a hand through his hair. "She was in a coma for four fucking years, Maddie. And everyone thought she was dead."

"I—um—"

"Her family planned a funeral. They buried her. They took *Jack*."

And she'd been alive the whole time.

"I—" I sucked in a breath, tried to release it, but it just stuck in my lungs. "I-I—how the fuck does something like that happen?"

"There was another woman in the accident."

I froze. "Oh my God."

"Apparently, the body Carrie's family buried wasn't her,

wasn't—" His eyes closed. "Of course, it wasn't her," he whispered. "She's alive and here."

I blinked. Once. Twice. "That's..."

Just seriously, *how the fuck could that happen?*

Ro's eyes opened. "So, while Carrie was fighting for her life as a Jane Doe, and her family was grieving, I-I...didn't do anything."

I shuddered, the idea of languishing in a hospital bed while unconscious for so long creeping me the fuck out. "How could you do anything, honey?" I said, pushing that away. "You didn't know. Nobody did."

And the universe better believe I'd be doing a post-mortem on this—

Another shudder.

Wrong choice of words.

"I *should* have known."

I weaved my fingers into his hair, drew him against me for a long, long moment. "You couldn't have known."

"I know." A beat. "And yet I can't help but know that I failed her."

"What?" I released his hair, leaned back enough to see his face. "How could you have possibly failed her?"

"I failed her by not finding out." He shoved his free hand through his hair, clenched at the strands, his body so tense beneath mine that it seemed impossible he was flesh and blood, seemed like he *had* to be made out of steel and granite. "Worse, I failed *Jack,* and Christ, baby, that's the one thing I can't live with. I fucking *can't—*"

He didn't fail them, not in the least.

He'd fought for Jack, fought for his son when so many other people would have given up.

But I didn't think he'd hear *that* right then, didn't think he would absorb it.

So, instead, I asked something I thought was equally as important. "We all let the people we love down, honey. We all mess up.

No one is infallible." Not even me, as hard as I tried. "So, why does it kill you to think that you failed Jack?"

His teeth *clicked* together so quickly my own jaw ached in sympathy, whatever protest that had forming on his tongue lost in the action.

"Ro."

"Never mind," he muttered. "You're right. We all fuck up. Of course we do."

"*Rome.*"

His hands went to my waist, and he started to lift me like he was going to set me out of his lap, set me away from him.

Since I knew all about strategic retreat, I was able to evade his, clutching at his shoulders, shifting so that I was straddling him further. This hiked up my skirt—it was either that or it was going to rip—but I supposed that wouldn't be the worst thing.

Because this was part of my plan.

Sidestep the retreat.

Distracting him with—

His palm settled on the bare skin of my thigh.

I shivered.

Maybe distracting *me*.

Mostly because his fingers had begun massaging the bare skin of my thigh, reminding me how very good we were together and that it had been a couple of days and—

His head dropped, teeth finding the lobe of my ear, nibbling.

Making me shiver, heat growing between my thighs. And moisture—enough that my underwear was immediately soaked.

I held on to my control, barely.

Focused, barely.

"Why would failing Jack kill you, honey?" I asked.

Because the way he'd said it, the way he was running from it, told me it was a fuck-ton more serious than normal parental worry.

He shook his head.

I cupped his cheek, drew his face back to mine. "Tell me."

His eyes closed for a long moment.

Then opened.

"My dad taught me that one thing is important."

I pivoted with the change in subject, even though that was something I hadn't expected him to say. All I knew about the Hutchins patriarch was that he had been beloved by his kids, by his wife, that his loss had left a heavy impact on everyone who'd loved him.

And on Ro too, apparently.

"What did he teach you?"

"To be there for and protect the people you love." His jaw flexed. "And I didn't do that."

"Honey," I whispered.

"And he'd be so fucking disappointed in me."

A knife to my chest. Because the way he said that fucking *destroyed* me.

"Look at the man you've become, honey," I murmured, struggling to find the right thing to say, to find something that would make him feel better, something that would take away his pain. "Of course he wouldn't be disappointed in you."

"You can't know what that's like," he rasped.

"What do you mean?"

His palm flattened on my thigh. "You're strong and capable and amazing." He shook his head. "I don't think you could have ever disappointed anyone."

He didn't know.

I'd told Jack the most of anyone, Mel the second most.

But neither of them had the full story, and Ro didn't either.

So, he couldn't know that before him and Ash and Mel and all the Hutchins crew came into my life, *all* I knew was how to disappoint people. I learned that as a kid who wasn't much older than Jack.

Before my parents had died because they hadn't wanted me.

And after, when my grandparents hadn't wanted me. When none of my other living relatives had wanted me either.

I'd lost my parents, my home, my friends, the life I knew.

I'd lost my stability.

And then had been shipped off to boarding school—my physical needs accounted for, but not my emotional ones.

I'd never been to a Game Night, never went home for the holidays. Never had a birthday present mailed to me like the other kids or a care package. I didn't even leave during the summer. I stayed on campus and took extra classes.

That meant I'd graduated early, had gotten out on my own early.

But it also meant that I hadn't felt what was tearing Ro apart.

And I might have come across the first problem I didn't have the skills to solve.

# SEVENTEEN

Ro

"I don't think you could have ever disappointed anyone."
I meant the words, meant them to the very depths of my soul.

How could I not?

She *was* amazing and capable and kind and selfless and—

Wincing so slightly that I might not have noticed if not for the fact that our faces were just inches apart.

But she *did* wince, and that slight sign of pain erased the drama of the night.

Suddenly, Carrie didn't matter.

Suddenly, my failures weren't at the forefront of my mind.

This woman, who I knew was mine, who I was still trying to figure out how to make that happen—what with the rest of the shit that was happening—had winced.

Which meant she was hurting.

Which meant—

I needed to make it stop.

"Maddie," I whispered.

She started to push up from my lap, but I caught her, held her against me. "Well," she said, tone brusque and businesslike as she let me settle her back in, "it's good that we know what happened to Carrie. That means Jack has a concrete reason for why his mom wasn't here." She paused and met my eyes, but only for a fraction of a second before she was talking again, words coming a mile a minute. "That's really good. I mean he's been through a lot, but he doesn't have to wonder now, doesn't have to think that she'd willingly leave him." She swallowed, and there was that wince again. "That will mean a lot to him."

I paused, considered how the fuck I was going to get her to open up to me—this woman who'd gotten dressed and was ready to hit the door before I'd returned from the bathroom, who'd avoided me until she'd stepped in to fix my shit (again), who'd begrudgingly allowed me to take her to my bed—and not so we could fuck, because clearly she didn't have a problem with my dick —and had disappeared before I'd woken up.

And back to avoiding.

Avoiding me, avoiding getting too close.

But not avoiding Jack (since I'd gotten the report from my son that she'd visited while he was at Ash's).

And not avoiding wanting to solve my problems.

Donning her armor and keeping me at a distance...while hiding her own pain.

Seriously, how the fuck did I get past the lance she seemed to have pointed in my direction?

She spoke before I figured out a way to convince her to set it aside. "How long ago did Carrie wake up?"

I swallowed, cleared my throat, and forced out, "Two months."

"And she just...woke up?"

I nodded. "There's no medical explanation for it. One day, she was unconscious, and the next...she was awake. It took her a couple of weeks to rebuild her strength enough to be discharged from the nursing home she'd been transferred to and get the paperwork to fly home."

"Hard to get on a plane if you're dead."

Another nod. "So, she flew home, found that her mom—who'd been watching Jack while she went on what was supposed to be a short holiday—had died and Jack wasn't there."

Fuck, that had to be terrifying.

"God," Maddie whispered.

"Yeah," I agreed. "It took a while, but she tracked me down by going through the paperwork from the custody battle—or tracked Ash's house down, anyway, since I'd used his address originally while my house was being built."

"And by the time she finally knocked on the door she was distraught," Maddie murmured, expression stark, eyes glimmering, her heart clearly aching for Carrie.

That didn't excuse the scene my ex had made, didn't excuse the scratches on my face. I just...could imagine how close to the edge I would be if that happened to me, if I woke up and my son was gone, in a foreign country, with a man I'd left without a word.

"Did she..." Maddie pressed her lips together, shook her head.

"What?"

Another wince, but this one didn't speak of old pain. It was sympathy for me. "Did she say why she left in the first place?"

My stomach twisted, and I shook my head. "No, baby." I sighed. "Aside from her mentioning that she had dual citizenship between the two countries, we didn't get to that part."

It explained how she got here so easily, how she'd packed up and left so quickly eight years ago.

But it didn't explain to me why she'd left in the first place.

I wanted that explanation, but there'd been too much other stuff to process.

"I'm sorry," Maddie murmured.

"I know." I wanted the explanation, but I could be patient

now, especially since I'd finally gotten *some* answers. The rest would come.

I hoped.

And right. So now I'd shared, I'd opened up to my woman, but I needed to understand something else.

Why Maddie seemed like she was in pain.

It was buried, hidden with capability and smiles and a no-nonsense, get-shit-done attitude, but beneath that façade was a vast, yawning crevice...disguising the deep vein of pain below.

"I don't want to talk about Carrie," I said softly.

There.

*Right* there.

Panic in pretty blue eyes.

I inhaled silently, held it, tried to figure out a way past her defenses...then decided that, ultimately, the only move she might not predict was one out of her own playbook.

Slowly, I slid my palm up her bare thigh, inching it beneath her skirt, skating along the edge of her underwear, slipping it beneath, gently teasing along the soaking wet lips of her pussy, then through it, drifting up toward her clit. "Why did you wince when I said you didn't disappoint people, baby?"

She shivered, but then my question hit and she blinked. "Wh-what?"

I circled her clit then pressed. She bucked against me, and I used my free hand to steady her for a moment...

Before slipping it beneath her skirt and dragging her panties down.

"You heard me, baby," I said, circling again, dancing my fingers in and then out, toward where she wanted them, then away.

Teasing.

"I don't know what you're talking about," she snapped.

I tsked. "Yes, you do. Why are you hurting?" I pressed again, this time with my thumb, this time not backing away, not teasing, and not giving her a reprieve. "What are you hiding?" I murmured, slipping a finger inside the tight sheath of her, curling it upward.

Her lips parted on a gasp. "Nothing," she said. "I'm an open book."

I almost laughed.

"So, why don't I really know anything about you?" I slid another finger in, began pumping them slowly in and out, in and out. "Why do I know the person you are inside, but don't have one fucking clue about the person you were before, about your past, about what made you this wonderful, amazing woman—"

"*Don't,*" she whispered, eyes pained, glistening with tears. "Please, don't."

I faltered, not wanting to be the one who caused her pain, not liking this tactic.

My stroking slowed, hand sliding down.

She grabbed at my wrist, pushing it up while wiggling down, impaling herself on my fingers. "Don't stop," she groaned, eyes sliding closed. "Please don't stop."

I sucked in a breath, debating.

But ultimately, I couldn't deny this woman anything.

So, I kept stroking her, doing it with purpose, without teasing, driving her up to an orgasm. But just as she crested that peak, the question slipped from my lips. "Why don't I know you, Maddie?"

She cried out, pussy rippling, my name on her tongue, her hips bucking as she ground down at me, her forehead dropping onto my shoulder, breaths puffing on my neck.

I didn't expect her to answer.

But she did.

"Because you won't like the person I am inside," she said so quietly I had to strain to hear her. "And then you'll leave."

My heart rolled over in my chest.

"Baby," I rasped.

She stiffened, head lifting, eyes going wide.

As though she hadn't meant to say that out loud.

"Baby—"

Her office phone rang, and we both turned to look at it.

"I need to take that call," she whispered, not meeting my eyes. "The team is waiting for me to join them."

My fingers were buried deep in her cunt, those tight internal muscles of hers still convulsing around me. I slid them out slowly, cock twitching when her mouth formed a silent protest and I debated pushing this.

But only for a second.

Because I knew I'd pushed far enough.

"Answer your phone, baby," I said, as it rang again, lifting her off my lap, tugging her panties back up, then holding her around the waist, waiting until she was steady.

Waiting until she—still not looking at me—walked around her desk again.

Waiting until she picked up the receiver. "Hello?"

Waiting until her eyes drifted back to mine and I saw that vein of hurt was a little closer to the surface.

I vowed to dig it out.

Only *then* did I go home.

# EIGHTEEN

## MADDIE

"You heading out of here soon?"

I glanced up, eyes slightly blurry from the hours I'd spent in my spreadsheets and docs, building a transition document.

Transition...because I needed to start the job Brooks had offered me.

So, that meant I needed to get my ducks in a row so someone else could step into my position and Ash's company would be okay and—

So that Ash would be okay.

I hit the buttons on my keyboard to save my work—something I did obsessively because the idea of losing anything (even though it was saved on the cloud) gave me hives and then glanced up at Ash, seeing him leaning back against the doorframe, arms crossed, eyes lasered in on me.

"Yeah," I said quickly. "I'm just going to finish this doc up and head out."

A lie.

I'd be here for hours, if only to avoid going back to my empty hotel room, to avoid doing something stupid like driving to Ro's house and...

Doing something stupid.

I'd told him—

*God*, I'd *told* him.

Too much. Too fucking much.

Ash studied me. "You've been working a lot."

I smiled. "I *always* work a lot." I shrugged. "It's kind of my thing."

That would usually make him smile back at me. But today it didn't. Today it had him pushing off the wall, taking a step into my office. "Are you okay?" he asked softly. "I know you don't like to share about yourself." Still quiet as he took a step closer. "But just tell me this much. Are you okay?"

"I'm fine."

It was a quick, bright statement...and one he didn't believe in the fucking *least*.

This illustrated by the fact that he crossed the room, rounded my desk, and cupped my jaw. "I'm here," he said softly. "Anytime. For anything."

Arrows to the heart.

One. Two. *Thunk. Thunk.*

I absorbed the blows, trying to think of something, *anything* to say, but...I didn't have to.

Ash dropped his hand, stepped back. "I want to see you for Game Night at Cora's, yeah?"

Three days from then. A deadline for me, but enough time for me to get my shit (and shields) together.

And God, he was such a good guy.

I was going to miss him when he got sick of my shit and cut ties.

Which would probably not be long after I left this job in someone else's hands.

Which begged the question of *why* I had accepted another position, why I was planning my departure with such razor-sharp focus.

"Maddie?"

I shook myself. "Yeah," I said softly. "I'll be there."

"Good." A nod, another touch to my cheek, and then he was gone. I went back to work, using it to distracted me from the view of Ash walking away, from the slice of pain that had gone through me at the sight.

I lost myself in cells and finicky company policy and tiny details of my job, saving my work at regular intervals because...anxiety.

Sometime later, my cell rang, and I reached over, picked it up. "Hello?

"Maddie?"

My body stiffened at the sound of Jack's voice.

I'd given him my number, told him to call any time he needed me.

But he hadn't (and neither had Ro, for that matter—which told me all I needed to know). And Christ, why was my brain such a fucking mess?

Ever since—

Well, since *ever.*

"Hello?" Jack's voice trembled on the question and I felt like an asshole, so wrapped up in my own disaster of a brain that I hadn't answered him.

"I'm here," I said quickly, getting the fuck out of my own head. "Are you okay?"

The resultant pause to my question had me up and out of my chair. "Where are you?" I asked.

"At home."

"Where's your sitter?"

Everyone in Rome's family was close to Jack and he spent lots of time at Ash and Mel's, but Ro had still hired someone to pick

Jack up from school and watch him until he got home from work a few days a week.

"She's downstairs. But, Maddie—"

My heart clenched, and I was already standing, already grabbing my purse and heading for the door. "What, honey?" I asked, pounding down the steps, waving to our security guy, Tim, and pushing out the door.

"I need cupcakes for class tomorrow, and she won't help me make them."

My panic receded slightly. "Cupcakes."

"For the bake sale and I forgot to tell Dad. And Tricia"—the sitter—"says she doesn't know how to make them, and that I wouldn't want her to bake them because she burns everything." His voice wobbled. "I can't have burned cupcakes."

I thought about offering to send Tricia some money so she could buy him some cupcakes. That would let me go back inside and finish what I needed to finish.

But I'd reached my car.

And I couldn't imagine telling Jack that.

He'd called me.

Which meant he needed something more. He needed *me*.

So, I didn't say anything about buying cupcakes or calling Mel to see if she had time to make them. I just said, "I'll stop at the grocery store, and then I'll be right there."

And I went *right* there.

After that quick stop at the store.

Not for premade cupcakes—though, on another day, I'd be down for them (there was something about the frosting they put on grocery store cupcakes that was just chef's kiss). But today I didn't go for premade. Instead, I bought ingredients to make my devil's food cake, knowing it would rock as cupcakes, knowing exactly what I needed because I'd made the recipe at Ro's place a couple of weeks ago, and...knowing it was easy enough that Jack could do most of it with my help.

Building his confidence.

Being there for him.

Everything I'd always dreamed of and...

Everything I'd never had.

My eyes teared up as I loaded the tin of cocoa powder into my reusable bag, but I just blinked them back, exhaled and grabbed the bars of chocolate, the bags of flour, the cupcake wrappers, packing those away as well. I'd been in Ro's pantry, knew that it was sparse on the baking front.

I'd fix that.

Like I'd fix everything else.

Then I'd go back to Europe, move on to Brooks's company.

Things would be like they always were—me visiting, me on the periphery, me part of the circle of these people I loved, but not in so deep they'd realize they were sick of me, tired of me, that they no longer *wanted* me.

Things would be normal.

# Nineteen

## Ro

"Oops," I heard as I pushed through the door and into the mudroom off the garage.

I paused then, having been a parent long enough to know that the tone of the *oops* wasn't a good sign, sped up, moving down the hall, intending to relieve Tricia from whatever chaos that Jack was creating.

Jack, with whom I'd reached a semi-tentative peace—this because of Maddie, of course. Those tickets to the soccer game, the VIP experience she'd had a hand in getting Jack, had worked some kind of magic, even though I'd mentioned Maddie had gotten them for us.

I couldn't lie to my son about that.

And...I think in telling him that, in not trying to take credit for shit I hadn't done, he'd thawed.

No more fights at school.

No complaints about homework or getting off his video games.

No more telling me he hated me.

We were going on almost a week of me not hearing the H-word.

So, I didn't need to lose my babysitter and throw a wrench into the whole system, not when it was finally working.

Only, when I moved into the kitchen, it wasn't to see Tricia cleaning up some chaos that Jack had created.

It was to see Jack and Maddie creating chaos *together*.

I froze, almost staggered back, my heart thudding, my head spinning.

"That's okay," Maddie said, reaching around Jack and using her hands to guide his as they—I leaned to the side—piped frosting onto the top of a cupcake. "Just like that," she was saying. "Slow and steady wins the race."

Jack nodded, fully focused, teeth nibbling into his bottom lip as, together, they carefully squirted frosting onto the cupcake.

"There," Maddie said, releasing his hands. "Ready to try the next one on your own?"

Jack, still nibbling at that lip, nodded.

Maddie moved a cupcake toward Jack. "Okay, bud," she said softly. "Give it a try on this one."

Another nod. Supreme focus.

And as I stood there, heart pounding, watching Maddie help my son ice a cupcake, watching her encourage him to do one on his own, watching them just have a quiet, normal moment, I was rocked to my core.

Because *this* was everything I'd ever wanted.

A family of my own.

Walking into my kitchen after being at work and seeing the woman I loved with my kid, smiling and sharing a moment—

Jack groaned. "That one looks terrible."

"We can fix it," Maddie said, picking up a butter knife and smoothing it over the surface. "See?"

"Whoa."

"Sometimes the best things aren't what we planned."

Jack paused, seemed to take that in. A second later, he glanced up at her and smiled. "Can we put sprinkles on them?"

Maddie smiled back. Then she reached over and tapped his nose, leaving a dollop of frosting. "Absolutely."

Jack scooped the dollop off, plunked his finger in his mouth, and I watched, heart squeezing, as he did the same to Maddie, breaking into peals of laughter at the sight of her with chocolate icing on the tip of her nose.

She waggled her brows as she wiped it off, licking it from the tip of her finger. "Tasty."

Jack laughed again.

But Maddie didn't.

Because maybe I'd made a sound, or maybe she just finally caught sight of me out of the corner of her eye, or maybe she just finally sensed that she wasn't alone. Either way, she spun slowly, lips parting, skin going pale then pink in her cheeks.

My woman. My kids in the kitchen. Laughter in the air.

*That* was all I'd dreamed of.

All I'd ever wanted. And I knew now, it was everything I'd ever needed.

"Hi," I said when she didn't speak.

Her throat worked. Once. Twice. Then she whispered, "Hi" in return.

Jack turned, and fuck if my vision didn't mist when his face lit up. When he actually looked happy to see me for a change. When he held up the icing bag. "Look what Maddie taught me how to do!"

My heart squeezed. My throat grew tight.

Because this was what my dad would have come home to, this was what had made my dad happy.

Then I shoved down the emotion stuck in the back of my throat and walked over to my son, walked over to Maddie, seeing the spread of cupcakes, most of them topped with thick, chocolatey frosting.

"Devil's food cake?" I asked.

Jack bounced up and down. "Yup! Maddie even let me crack the eggs."

"Really?"

An energetic nod, my son excited and acting like a seven-year-old, not a traumatized, angry kid who couldn't stand to look at me. "And I melted the chocolate without burning it!"

"That's amazing," I told him honestly. "I don't think I could do that."

"I could show you," he offered.

"I'd like that." Was it raspy as fuck and maybe edged with the slightest hint of water?

Yeah.

But I didn't care.

Because this was my son, my dream...my eyes slid to Maddie's... my woman.

She'd taken the piping bag back from Jack and now had her head bent over the bowl, scooping frosting into the clear plastic bag.

"Maddie," I murmured.

Her shoulders hitched up, just slightly, but eventually she looked at me. I wanted to thank her for giving me this gift. I wanted to take her in my arms, hold her close, tell her how much it meant. I wanted to smear that frosting all over her naked skin and lick it off, making her come until she was so limp with pleasure she couldn't move.

But obviously, I couldn't do any of that.

So I just said, "You've got frosting on your nose."

Teeth in her bottom lip, cheeks going even pinker, eyes dancing...

I swiped my thumb over her nose, lifted it to my mouth and tasted that frosting, watched her lips part, her eyes go...

Hot and needy.

"It's good, right, Dad?"

Pushing hot and needy out of my mind—because my kid was *right there*—I tore my gaze from Maddie's and turned to Jack. "Yeah, bud. It's really good."

Raspy again, but for a whole different reason.

I exhaled, opened my mouth—

Maddie's arm appeared in front of my face as she passed the bag over to Jack. "Here you go, bud. Want to demonstrate one and then your dad can try?"

"Okay!" Jack demonstrated...and, fuck, if my kid didn't pipe that frosting on top like a goddamned professional.

And maybe that was Dad Pride speaking.

But I didn't even care.

Not when my son was looking up at me with excitement instead of hatred in his eyes and teaching me something and—

We were here. Now.

Having this moment.

*Another* moment that Maddie had created.

Maddie.

*My* Maddie.

I turned, wanting to draw her close, to show her what Jack had done because of her, to feel her body against mine and tempt her into another tease of that chocolate on her skin and my tongue.

But when I rotated around...

She was gone.

Spinning further, I saw the room was empty.

I turned back to Jack...just as I heard a soft rumble. My eyes flashed up from the cupcakes, up and out the window, seeing the flash of headlights.

Knowing that it belonged to Maddie's car.

Running.

Again.

"Ready to try, Dad?"

I blinked, shoved down the urge to chase after her, to make her tell me why the fuck she kept running anytime we drew close, why the fuck she thought I wouldn't like the person she was inside.

How that could even be possible when she'd given me all of *this*.

Knowing I needed to dig that out.

Knowing I needed to make her see that what she feared was impossible.

But...I needed to finish making these cupcakes with my son first.

And then there would be no more giving her space, no more waiting for her to get comfortable, no more trying to be respectful of the walls she continued to erect.

Because I was about to burst through that shit like the fucking Kool-Aid man.

# TWENTY

## MADDIE

I hit the button to save, then closed the document, knowing I was going into a level of detail that was completely unnecessary but unable to get myself to stop.

I needed to make sure my replacement was up to snuff.

And maybe...fuck, I couldn't even believe I was admitting this to myself, but maybe I was delaying, going into such detail so I could stay longer.

I *had* to leave.

I just...maybe I could stay a bit longer.

There was so much work to do, after all.

I opened the document back up, went to the last paragraph I'd just finished inputting and scoured the lines for where I could add more detail—

"Maddie!"

Glancing past my monitor, I saw that Jack was standing in my office doorway. He was wearing a soccer uniform with socks pulled up to his knees, the straps from his backpack thin and black on his shoulders, like it was one of those bag ones that tightened at the top before it turned into an actual backpack.

"Hey, bud," I said, pushing my chair back and standing up, crossing over to him. "You have a game tonight?"

A nod. "Wanna come?"

"I—"

"Dad said I could invite anyone I wanted, so I invited my mom—"

I felt my eyes go wide.

"—and she's going to come."

They went a little wider, but I shouldn't be surprised. Ro had answers. Carrie was here now. Going to one of Jack's games was a good start and reinitiating contact in a safe—and public—place. I approved.

"That's really good, bud. I'm sure she'll love watching you play."

"Yup." He popped the p. "So, are you going to come too?"

"It sounds like it might be a kind of special time with your mom," I said softly. "Are you sure you want me there?"

He hesitated for a second—and I got it then, identified with the flash of hesitation, with the fact that he wanted another person he was comfortable with there. Someone who *got* it. For whatever reason, the universe had ensured we had a bond, a connection that was deeper than it should be considering how short of a time we'd spent together.

But he was a good kid.

And I could understand that he'd feel insecure about this first meeting with his mom after that scene the other day.

I'd told him about feeling lost and unwanted.

I didn't tell him those emotions were branded on my soul.

Because I didn't want him to feel like that was his future.

So, really, I couldn't *not* be there for him.

"Because I'd love to come," I said before he could take the invite back. "If you really want me there."

He nodded quickly.

"Then I'll be there—"

I didn't even get to finish the sentence before he was closing the distance between us, before he was throwing his arms around me and hugging me tight. "Thanks, Maddie," he whispered.

How could I leave this?

The question sliced through my mind like a razor blade, indecision a thousand cuts on my heart.

Mostly because my answer was only,

*How could I not?*

———

"That's my baby!" Carrie shouted, fist pumping as she cheered loudly.

I was cheering my own head off, so damned excited about a rec soccer league game that it was almost embarrassing.

But Jack had gotten the ball and dribbled all the way up the field and scored the game-winning goal.

Okay, so they didn't keep score at this level and age, but *I'd* been keeping an accurate count in my head as the match progressed and Jack had put his team ahead approximately ten seconds before the ref blew the whistle to end the match.

So, yeah.

The kid kicked butt.

I grinned as he ran down the field, slapping hands with his teammates, smile wide and bright enough that I knew there was no way I was going to forget it.

Beautiful.

The happiness on his face was beautiful—

"I owe you an apology."

I tore my gaze from the field over to Carrie, who'd finished her cheering and was looking at me with somber eyes.

"For what?" I asked carefully, treading lightly.

"You know," she whispered. "I was a bitch to you, and I made a scene, and"—her throat worked—"I was just so panicked and worried and *relieved* and then Jack was there, in my arms. But he wasn't the same," she added softly. "He was bigger, not my little boy a-and I missed out on that. He's not the baby I left behind."

No, he wasn't.

"And I...after I woke up, I was a mess and then seeing that, seeing the reminder of all I'd lost out on—" She nibbled at the corner of her mouth. "I went a little insane."

I couldn't even begin to comprehend what that must have been like, how scary and heart-wrenching it must have been to go through it, but also...

"You did miss out on a lot," I said softly. "But so did Rome."

She winced, rocked back on her heels, eyes sliding away.

"Why did you leave?" I shook my head. "Never mind," I said quickly. "That's not an explanation you owe me." I held her eyes. "It's Rome who deserves to know."

Carrie glanced down at her hands. "I know he does, and...God, it's so stupid. I almost called him a hundred times after I left. I loved him, I really did. But the thought of getting married, of being stuck in the life he described he wanted...I couldn't do it," she murmured. "I *couldn't,* and I didn't know how to tell him and then he asked me to marry him and I...*snapped.*" She exhaled, glanced up and over my shoulder and I turned, saw that Ro had come up, his expression closed down, but his eyes—the hurt in them eviscerated me. "I didn't know I was pregnant then," Carrie said. "I know you probably don't believe me, but I wasn't sick and I was still getting my period. It wasn't until I actually went into labor that I realized what was happening, and then"—she sighed—"then what was I going to do? Jack was here and I loved him already and I couldn't just call you and tell you there was a baby—"

"Yes, you could have."

Ro's tone was...frosty, and I didn't blame him.

Jesus fuck. I mean, I appreciated that Carrie had reined it in, was here for Jack, was working to navigate her way forward with Ro. But who was to say that she wasn't just going to try to take him and disappear off into the sunset?

Carrie froze.

Then her chin dropped. "Yes," she whispered. "I could have. I *should* have. But I didn't know how to go back after I'd left and—"

"And what?" Ro asked when she didn't go on, stepping close to me, his palm resting on the small of my back.

"I wanted to go back, wanted to never have left."

Still behind me, Ro stiffened.

"I wanted that fairy tale you offered me, the family in the kitchen cooking together and laughing over a meal, Game Nights and unwavering support, a marriage where I had a man who loved me for me..."

Ro's hand convulsed, fingertips clenching into my back.

"I knew I could never go back, never fix what I'd broken," Carrie murmured. Then she sighed and shook her head. "I knew I could never have what I really wanted."

There was a long pause, the noise of the kids running around and indecipherable sound of people chatting near us filtering in.

But it was all distant.

All muted.

Because my pulse was pounding in my veins, in my ears.

"What did you really want, Carrie?" Ro asked quietly.

Another pause, this one longer and more tense than the previous one.

"You."

# Twenty-One

Ro

I reared back, realizing too late I'd been so taken by shock that I hadn't schooled my face.

But, seriously, fuck, was Carrie actually saying she wanted me, wanted to be with me...and then had stayed away for four more years?

What. The. Fuck?

The woman was either delusional or full of shit, and I didn't know if it was better to call her on that, ignore her, or try to change the subject to something that was significantly safer.

Like abortion rights.

Or nuclear war.

Or—

"Dad!"

My hand flexed on Maddie's back as Jack ran up and I had to resist the urge to tug him to my side, to draw him away from Carrie.

She'd tabled the psycho but the shit she'd just said...

I was worried that Psycho might make another appearance.

I hated what happened to her, hated that she'd suffered, but fuck if this entire situation wasn't of her own making.

We could have broken up. She *should* have told me about Jack.

It was simple as that.

And none of this would have happened and—

I shoved that down, turned to my son. "Nice goal, bud."

His face lit up so brightly that I lost my breath for a second. "Did you see it?" he asked.

"Of course I did," I told him, dropping my hand from Maddie's back and crouching in front of him. "I really liked how you looked for a pass and when you didn't have one, you took it up yourself."

"Really?"

"Yup." I ruffled his hair. "In fact, I like it so much that I think it means we can celebrate with pizza."

"*Really?*"

I grinned, glad that Carrie was back—even with all the other bullshit she was spinning—*so fucking* glad that Maddie was here, that Jack had them both and that I had a kid who was happy for the first time since I'd been lucky enough to get him.

"Really," I said.

"Can Mom and Maddie come?"

I saw Maddie jerk slightly out of the corner of my eye, didn't know—and didn't really give a fuck—what Carrie's response was. I just knew that I wanted more time with Maddie, more time when she couldn't run, so I nodded in answer to Jack's question. "Yup," I said. "They sure can."

"Do you want to come, Mom?"

I glanced up then, following Jack's stare.

Carrie looked like she was going to cry, but in a happy way. "Of course, baby boy. I would love to come."

Jack bounced a little on his cleats as he turned toward Maddie. "You're going to come too, right?"

Not asking.

Not really.

It was more in expectation.

He knew that Maddie would come through.

I watched a muscle in her cheek flex. "I'd love to come."

"Yes!" Jack bounced again, excitement in every cell, but I saw the panic in Maddie's eyes, panic that grew when he said, "This is the best day *ever!*"

Dig out whatever bullshit was in Maddie's mind and launch it into a fucking incinerator.

Burst through the walls she was throwing up, a la the Kool-Aid man.

But, first...assuage the panic.

"Want to take your mom," I said, "and go grab a snack and your bag?"

Jack nodded so fast I was surprised he didn't turn into a bobblehead. "Yeah," he said, grabbing Carrie's hand—to which I got another glimpse of almost happy tears from my ex's eyes—and taking off, dragging his mom behind him.

"And your water bottle!" I called.

Carrie lifted a hand, telling me she'd heard.

I turned toward Maddie, saw—yup—the panic was right there in the front of her mind.

"I should let you guys have dinner as a family—" she began, slipping back a step. "You need to keep working things out between you all and me being there—"

"I'm calling Mario's," I said, pulling out my cell, talking right over her, not acknowledging the bullshit she was shoveling in my direction. Yeah, Carrie and I had a shit-ton of work to do to navigate this fucked up situation, but there wasn't going to be any rekindling of a relationship, weren't going to be any second chances.

Not after everything.

Not after *Maddie.*

"Do you want the Spicy Veggie, cupcake?"

She floundered for a second.

And I knew why.

I was pulling out the big guns, tempting her with one of her favorite restaurants, with her favorite pizza, with her favorite type of food (carbs).

Devious.

But...channeling my inner Kool-Aid man.

"I—uh..." She swallowed. "You don't have to—"

I hit the number I had on speed dial and listened to it ring. "Hey, Mario," I said when the owner had answered. "It's Rome. Can I get a delivery to my place for a large Spicy Veggie, a kid's cheese, and garlic bread."

Another weakness of Maddie's.

Mainly because it was more carbs.

Like I said, devious.

Maddie groaned softly at the mention of garlic bread and I knew that I had her. Even if Jack let her off the hook—which he wouldn't.

He'd bonded with Maddie.

He wanted her there.

So...she would be there.

But garlic bread and Spicy Veggie pizza would seal the deal for getting her to my place.

Where I could commence digging.

And busting through walls.

———

"I can't believe how grown up he is," Carrie said softly, following me as we tiptoed from the room and quietly shut the door.

We'd been reading with Jack, exchanging pages on the book he needed to read for school, a thrilling tale of a boy and his dog that better not end in fucking heartbreak. Otherwise, I was going to go down to school and throw a fit and the damned teacher and principal were going to have to put *me* on a behavior plan.

Maddie had been quiet since I'd wrangled her into dinner.

Probably because Jack had talked her ear off on the way over to my place, and then through dinner, alive and vibrant in a way that was almost unrecognizable.

But it was more than that, I knew.

I could sense the tension coiling inside her, spiraling more and more by the second.

Sooner or later, it would snap, spring forward and—

I was going to catch it.

But I had to get Carrie out of here first.

We all headed down to the kitchen, and, as I could have predicted, I saw Maddie preparing to retreat. Luckily, I'd made plans (and a series of Plan B's) as we'd read.

"Well," she began. "I should let you two—"

"Cupcake," I said, and didn't miss Carrie deflating slightly, knowing that she might have said what she said at the park, but she was also picking up the very deliberate signals I was sending her way—namely that it didn't matter what she said because we were *over* and had been from the moment she'd disappeared from my life like she had, from the moment she'd decided to *stay* gone. "Ash sent over some paperwork he wanted you to review," I added when Maddie glanced my way. I tilted my head down the hall. "It's on my computer if you want to check it out."

"I—"

"Go on, baby," I murmured, stepping closer, running my hand up her side, bringing my lips very close to her ear. "I'll be in there as soon as I walk Carrie out."

"I—"

"Come on, Care," I said, straightening and moving toward the front door. I picked up my ex's purse and coat, barely resisted the urge to shove them in her arms as she walked toward me.

But I had *some* manners, helping her into her jacket, passing over her purse, standing in the open front door, watching as she made her way down to her car, got in, and drove away with a wave.

Knowing I had time because Maddie's car was at the office.

Because it wouldn't be easy for her to escape.

Because I was ready to bust through those walls.

# Twenty-Two

## Maddie

I frowned at the monitor, the screen locked and requiring a password.

Wondering why the heck Ash would send Ro some files.

A noise in the doorway had me glancing up, seeing the man of the hour moving into the space, moving around the desk, moving toward me. I expected him to lean against the heavy wooden top, to tell me the password so I could get to the files.

Instead, he pushed the chair back—and me along with it—and lifted me up, sitting in the desk chair then drawing me down onto his lap.

One of my favorite places to be.

And I'd only had it twice before.

I wanted it...forever.

"I need you to put in your password," I said, trying to shove that away, trying to put us back on task.

While sitting in his lap.

And doing it wanting to stay there forever.

This was going to work out fine. Totally *fine*.

His arms tightened, and he drew me more firmly against him, hand diving into my hair, tucking my head beneath his chin, pressing my ear to his chest, to the spot above his heart.

I was listening to the steady *thrum-thrum, thrum-thrum, thrum-thrum* of his pulse, so it took me a second to hear him when he said, "No, you don't."

No, I don't...need his password?

Stiffening, I started to sit up again.

His hand just slid along my side, holding me there. "No, cupcake," he murmured, "you don't need the password because Ash didn't send you any files."

"I—"

"But if you *want* the password, it's cinnamon."

Still trying to process the fact that Ro had lied about me having files waiting from Ash, I was sent reeling when he just dropped his password into the conversation casually, and then caught flat-footed about the fact that it was cinnamon.

That all spun around my head then stilled, pieced together, my mind clearing.

"Not swirl?" I asked lightly.

A rough chuckle, the noise rumbling through his chest, settling in my heart. "Nope. Not swirl, baby."

My pussy convulsed, remembering the last time I'd sat in this chair and he'd called me baby and...

"Why did you lie?" I whispered.

His nose came to my hair, and he inhaled deeply. "How do you always get it to smell so fucking good?"

"I—" I was spinning again. I needed to focus on work. I wanted to distract him with sex. I *wanted* sex. I needed...I didn't know what I needed except to sort my head out and win the battle between panic and desire.

Distract. Orgasms. Run, run away.

Give him what he needed, give Jack what *he* needed, and...keep my heart safe.

"Dry shampoo," I blurted.

A beat. Then, "What's that?"

"It's a spray that—" I cut myself off before I could break down the merits of not having to wash my hair, while it not looking like a greasy mess and apparently leaving it smelling *so fucking good*. "Why did you lie about the files?"

"To get you to stay."

I'd wanted him to answer the question, but I hadn't expected that bald statement.

My throat tightened. "You should spend time with Carrie, work on rebuilding the family you both want."

"I do want a family," he murmured, his arms tightening. "But I don't want it with Carrie."

I jerked, shoved hard against his chest, and I must have taken him by surprise with the sudden movement because I toppled from his lap, sucking in a breath and bracing, thinking I was going to hit the edge of the desk, the carpet below.

But then he was cursing, reaching for me, yanking me back.

The chair slammed against the wall, I collided with his chest, and he broke my fall.

Wincing, I opened my mouth. "I'm—"

In a second, our positions were reversed and I was flipped onto my back, Ro pressed into me from stomach to thigh, pinning me in place.

"I'm sorry," I whispered.

His mouth dropped down, our breaths intermingling. "Don't *fucking* apologize."

Inhaling, I tried to think of something to say. And failed.

Because what *was* there to say besides sorry?

Or maybe to tell him how fucking good it felt to be beneath him—something that would be better without the layers of clothes between us.

"I don't *want* Carrie," he growled.

"Okay," I said, still whispering, tabling my thoughts of naked fun time.

"I want *you*."

That sent my heart rolling in my chest, my lungs going tight, disquiet gathering in my abdomen. My desire disintegrated and suddenly I wanted to be anywhere but where I was, anywhere but pinned in place, his stare locked onto mine, knowing with a growing sense of dread that everything between us was about to go wrong.

"But I know I can't have you unless you talk to me," he said softly.

Yup.

Wrong. So fucking *fucking* wrong.

I couldn't talk to him. I couldn't explain. I—

"Why do you spend your life taking care of everyone else, working your magic, killing yourself for them, and you don't think you deserve the same in return?"

My head was already shaking. I couldn't go down that road, couldn't think that, could—

His palm came to my jaw, turning my face back to his. "Why do you think that you're not worthy of someone loving you?"

Tears in my eyes, dripping down my cheeks, but I just shook my head again.

"Why do you think that, for as much as I love the woman you present to the world, I couldn't love the person you are inside?"

Oh God, I couldn't handle this.

I pushed at his chest. "I need to go. I need—"

He cupped my jaw again, held me fast. "You *need* to tell me."

"I—"

"Tell me."

"I—"

"Baby," he ordered, "just fucking *tell me*."

"When you see the real me," I blurted, "you'll *know* that I'm not worthy of devotion, of killing yourself for me. You'll see that I'm just a stupid girl with stupid hopes and no chance of being loved—"

"Baby." His voice was a rasp now, face gentling, eyes filling with concern.

But the words were coming, and there was no sticking my finger in the dam, no way to stop the flow. They were gushing out and tearing through every barrier I'd created to keep them contained. "And that's not just bullshit low self-esteem talking," I snapped, sitting up, forcing him back onto his knees. "That's a *fact*. Not once in my life has someone loved me for me. My parents were wrapped up in their lives, their love, and never had time for me. I was always too loud, too much trouble, too big of an intrusion on their lives. And after they died, not one family member wanted me, did you know that?" I blew out a breath and shook my head. "Not *one*. Eventually, the social workers got them to take pity on me so I didn't end up in the system. But do you know how long I lasted at their house?"

Solemn, he shook his head.

"For two weeks."

"Fuck, baby."

"I was a grieving little girl, not sure of my place in the world, hoping against hope that this might be my chance at finding people to love me and—" I sighed. "They shipped me off to boarding school. They wouldn't let me come home for the holidays, paid through the nose to keep me there during the summer. You know why?"

Another solemn shake of my head.

"Because they'd rather pay to have me stay away from them than include me in their lives, their families."

"Cupcake—"

"*All* of them—my parents, my aunts and uncles, my grandparents. Not one of them could summon a modicum of love." I laughed, but it was ragged. "So what does that say about me? That there's something so wrong with me, something so incredibly messed up, something so damned *broken* that I know I can never, *ever* have something like what you describe."

# Twenty-Three

Ro

"Bullshit."

I saw her rear back, saw the shock register on her face.

"Wh-what?" she whispered.

"That's complete and total bullshit."

Anger flashed in her eyes. "I lived that fucking life. It's not bullshit."

"Baby," I told her, sitting back onto my ass and drawing her into my lap. "I'm not denying that you lived through a nightmare." Or that I wanted to track down those family members and make sure they experienced a far worse fate than what they'd subjected an innocent little girl to. It was just...

Maddie's past was a convenient excuse.

Because she was scared, fucking scared out of her mind, and *that* was why she kept throwing up roadblocks.

She just...needed to see it.

"You lived through something awful, something you never should have had to experience." I ran my hand through her hair, tilting her head back, holding her eyes with mine. "Too much, baby, and I hate that. I wish I could change that."

A tear slid down her cheek, and I brushed it away.

"But I can't and neither can you and..." I pressed my lips to her forehead. "That's not what's holding you back now."

Her lips parted on a shaking exhale.

"You're scared."

She went stiff, so fucking stiff that I knew everything I'd been putting together, all the puzzle pieces I'd been lining up in my mind were right.

"You're terrified."

She inhaled.

"Terrified that if you love me, you'll be hurt again. And you've been *so* hurt, baby, so fucking hurt that you can't risk it." I touched her cheek. "I get that. I felt some small piece of that after Carrie had left me, after I'd closed down, after you came back into my life and I realized what was in my heart. I just..." I tucked her hair behind her ear. "What I feel for you is bigger than the fear."

That air slid out of her in a hiss. "Ro."

I pressed my hand to her chest, feeling her heart pound beneath it. "So, you need to figure out what you feel here and if I'm worth it. Worth the risk, worth the potential for heartbreak, worth the gloriousness of the life we can build together."

"I—*shit*," she whispered, a tear clinging to her lashes.

"Worth the love that can grow between us."

She shuddered.

"Because, *God*, I could fucking love you."

More tears. More shaky breaths. More scared, sad eyes on mine as I waited for that to sink in, for her to decide.

If I was worth more than the fear.

"I like you, honey," she murmured. "So much."

Relief coating every inch of my soul.

"But there's no point in doing this," she said, shattering me into a thousand tiny pieces. "Because I'm leaving anyway."

---

I'd been so deep in relief I didn't hear it at first.

Then I did.

*"I'm leaving anyway."*

What the fu—

"So, we just need to live in the now," she said and turned her head, sealing her mouth over mine before I had a chance to sit in *that* fucked-up statement.

I kissed her back, because it was Maddie and I always wanted to kiss her, because her lips on mine were fucking perfect—and add in her body below mine, her curves soft and lush, her tongue slipping into my mouth, and it was the best kind of distraction.

Only...I didn't *want* to be distracted.

"No," I said, lifting my head, knocking her hands from my hair, setting her away, settling her on the rug next to me, keeping my mind safe from those delicious, dangerous curves.

"Honey," she murmured, leaning back into me. "I *want* you."

Fuck.

I wanted her too—wanted to be stroking into her slick heat, feel the clasp of her cunt around my dick. I wanted to taste my name on her lips, to feel her nails bite into my skin. I wanted to fuck her until we both couldn't stand.

But this was more important.

So, when her lips hit mine a second time, I jerked back, catching her shoulders and keeping her at a distance, hating that space, but hating more the expression on her face.

The *hurt*.

But, again, this was more important.

"No," I said, holding her fast.

"What do you want from me?" she asked, lips swollen, breaths coming in rapid succession.

"Not *that*," I snapped, pissed and turned the fuck on and *pissed*. "And I already told you, baby."

Panic on her face.

Her gaze sliding away.

Telling me that she was too deep in the fear to choose me.

Which hurt, but fuck, I knew this wasn't something that would change like the flip of the switch. I could give her time to consider and think and—

She was leaving.

After the last few weeks with me and Jack, after the last few *years* helping me fight for my son, she was just going to fucking disappear again, just go back to flitting in and out of our lives like a goddamned hummingbird. No. A fairy who liked to sprinkle her magic and then disappeared when shit got real.

"I'll get you and Jack settled before I go," she said quietly.

My hold on my temper slipped. "Stop slipping in and working your magic like you're a fucking magical Fix-It Fairy and then vanishing when you catch feelings because you don't think you deserve to have people in your life who love you."

Her throat worked, eyes sliding away, voice quiet. "That was uncalled for."

I sighed, shoved a hand through my hair. "No, it's probably the most honest thing I've ever said to you."

She sucked in a breath, eyes darting around, panic in every inch of her. I'd pushed her a long way, probably too far, too fast. Getting her to share why she had those walls, barreling through them, digging out the past, laying a heavy truth on her, and now...this.

But I couldn't summon a fuck.

Probably because there was more to say.

So, I couldn't stop now.

"And you love all of us Hutchinses," I snapped.

That breath hissed out.

"And you want to be here." Still snapping. "You want to be a real part of the family, be with me and Jack and not in whatever fucked-up way you think you deserve—a way that's full of half-measures and living on the outside and watching everyone else have what you want but are too scared to grab on to."

I paused then, watched her eyes fill with tears again, hating that she was hurt, but also knowing that if I didn't settle this right now, we would never get past it.

"So, you don't want to leave. You don't want to run. You want me." I stood, scooped her up, and carried her from the room, carrying her upstairs, dropping her into my bed, following her down. "You want me and Jack and the beauty we can create together."

She stared up at me with wide eyes.

"You want a family." I softened my voice, dropped my forehead against hers. "You *know* you do."

"I..." Her eyes slid closed. "I don't know what I want."

"No. You *know*, baby. You're just too scared right now to see it." I cupped her jaw. "I can give you time, but I can't give you space to find it. I need you to trust me to see you through to the other side of this, trust me to keep you safe, to protect your heart and mind and soul. Trust me to love you."

Silence.

Long and drawn out, her eyes closing, hiding the turmoil I knew had to be happening in her mind.

Silence for so long I knew I had to pull out my trump card.

"I spent years mourning for a woman who didn't want me as I am, who didn't trust me. Who *left*." Her eyes opened, hurt in them all over again—but this time that pain was for me. "It was agony, cupcake—that she didn't want that with me or couldn't allow herself to have it, or just...changed her mind. It hurt so much that, as much as I know it's different with you, know that we have the potential of something that's so much more than Carrie and I could have ever made, I know that I can't do it unless you're all in."

She paled. "So, I can give you time to think, to come to terms with all I dropped on you, with the emotions in your mind and heart, but I can't make us work unless you make an effort. Unless you have staying power. Unless you're as much committed to me as I'm going to commit to you. Because baby, if I give you my heart, you'd fucking better be in my arms in the morning when I wake up."

# Twenty-Four

MADDIE

He was on top of me, pouring out his heart.

Eviscerating me.

And...I didn't know if I could fix this.

Didn't know if I could give him what he wanted.

Because he said that was me, and I just...didn't believe it.

Because he hadn't changed when I told him about those deep secrets in my heart, the painful parts of my past. All my hidden fears exposed for the world, and he'd held me close and touched me gently and, yeah, maybe his face had changed, maybe he'd felt for me, hurt for me, gotten frustrated because I wouldn't just give in.

But beneath that all, he was Rome.

And...I wanted to be there when he woke up in the morning, wanted to be the woman who held and protected his heart.

I wanted it so badly, I could almost taste it.

I just...didn't know if I could take that first bite.

"There it is," he said softly.

My eyes flew back to his, and I hadn't even realized that I was looking away, that I was falling back into the pit of panic and fear again.

"Yeah, cupcake," he murmured, "you're seeing it now, aren't you?"

That I was living my life in fear?

"That's not something I need to see," I snapped. "I've lived it for thirty-odd years."

Strangely enough, my show of temper had him grinning.

"What?" I asked, still snapping. "What's so fucking funny?"

"You." He bent, kissed the tip of my nose. "Because you hate it."

My pulse picked up. "I'm happy in my life. Work fulfills me and I—"

"Hate that you're afraid. Hate that you're too scared to leap. You work so fucking hard to be capable at everything, to do each and every task perfectly so no one can find fault in you, but"—his thumb brushed lightly over my bottom lip, the tender touch filling my stomach with butterflies—"you want more."

I inhaled sharply.

He was fucking right, dammit.

And I didn't want to think about it...because then I'd be stepping out from behind my huge, steel shield, because then I would be exposed and vulnerable and—

I shivered slightly because the room was cold.

Or maybe that was the chill deep inside my heart.

Beckoning me down into the abyss.

"I *want* orgasms," I muttered, pushing that thought away.

His mouth curved. "And I want to give them to you, baby, but not until you come to the Light Side. Not until you don't need to use sex to distract and keep me out of that beautiful heart of yours. Not until you leap and trust that I'll catch you." He stood up like he hadn't just dropped a bomb on me, undressing us both down to our underwear, unclipping my bra and tossing it to the side. He pulled his shirt over my head then tugged back the covers, crawling in beside me before he brought them over both of us. And seriously, if that little show of care hadn't undone me, the way he gently—oh so gently—took me in his arms, holding me tight, inhaling the scent of my hair positively wrecked me.

"It's supposed to be Dark Side," I grumbled, even as I took another step toward the edge of that chasm.

"No, cupcake." He kissed the top of the head. "Enough dark. We're going to start living in the light."

———

I woke in his arms in the morning.

It was early, the first rays of the sun just beginning to creep over the horizon, but that was a distant thought.

Because I'd woken with Ro's fingers stroking through my pussy.

"Oh. God," I whispered.

He rolled over the top of me, hair mussed, eyes sleepy and heated, but his smile was pure sin. "You stayed, baby."

I'd stayed.

Terrified half out of my mind, I'd wanted to slip out, wanted to run as I'd stared into the darkness with Ro's arms around me. He'd taken a long time to fall asleep, but I'd taken longer, not able to drift off until exhaustion swept up and claimed me.

Now I was awake, desire building, my pussy already quivering, wanting his fingers to slip inside, to stroke me slow and deep, wanting him to follow with his cock, but harder and faster and deeper.

Right then, though, his thumb was circling my clit, teasing and easy and—

I arched my hips, wanting more contact, earning a chuckle in return. "I thought I didn't get orgasms until I declared my undying love."

Another chuckle. "Naughty."

I didn't get a chance to utter a snarky comment in response to that.

He pressed hard against my clit, making me gasp and buck against his hand. "You stayed, cupcake, so while I don't think you've come over completely to the Light Side, I think you deserve a little reward."

Yes.

I wanted that.

Wanted him.

Wanted to wake up to him doing this every day for the rest of my life.

His free hand swept up my side, beneath his T-shirt he'd put on me, closing in on—

I groaned when he palmed my breast, massaging my flesh, teasing my nipple, driving me slowly insane.

He plucked at my nipple, rolled the taut bud, sending wave after wave of bliss through me.

A beautiful fucking feeling.

And that wasn't even including what he was doing between my legs, sliding his fingers along my labia, using his thumb to tease my clit, stroking one thick finger into me, following it with another. Thumb and fingers working in tandem, shooting me toward the edge.

Then stopping with me hovering right at the peak.

It was then that he gave me more, built a tenuous bridge over to the Light Side, encouraging me across the wood and rope, holding the whole thing steady. He stripped me gently, trailing delicate kisses over my skin, rising over me, pausing only to take off his clothes, to grab a condom and roll it down the hard length of his cock.

Spreading my thighs, pushing inside.

Slow. Deep.

Looking me in the eyes the entire time.

And...tears clouded my vision as I crept across the bridge, held safe in his arms, trusting he'd keep me safe.

Not just sensation.

Not just painful, barbed need and memories clawing at the back of my mind.

This was joy and pleasure, hope and desire.

This was me putting the fear aside and...

Seeing what it could be like, the beautiful future this man had painted for me.

"This, baby," he murmured. "*This* is what you're going to fight for."

A tear escaped, clinging to my lashes for one long moment before it slipped free, slid down my cheek.

Ro wiped it free, continued those easy, steady thrusts, continued taking us up to the precipice together, continued loving me...

Until I exploded.

And was filled with glorious, beautiful pleasure.

And I was terrified.

And I was...still creeping across that narrow wooden bridge.

Knowing it was either toward the sweetest thing I could ever hope for...or that I was heading for a dark dive into oblivion.

# TWENTY-FIVE

RO

We'd showered together and I'd soaked in what Maddie was giving me, knowing it was the best gift ever, not wanting to let her go, but knowing that I needed to anyway.

We'd had an emotional night.

She'd shared and opened up.

Then this morning, making love with her beautiful blue eyes on mine, the tears sliding down her cheeks, knowing she was feeling what I was feeling...

She'd needed a little space to retreat and regroup and—

Think.

And I'd known that Jack would be up soon, would be in the kitchen wanting breakfast, or in my room talking to me as I got ready—something else that had never happened until Maddie had worked her magic.

My kid didn't need to come through the door and see a woman in my bed.

Though, he loved Maddie, would probably be thrilled for

more time with her.

We all just needed...kid gloves and careful steps forward.

And, honestly, Carrie was an issue.

Case in point, me walking up to my office building and seeing my ex standing outside the front doors. Waiting for me.

Not the woman I wanted showing up at my work out of the blue, that was for damned sure.

And not the woman I wanted at all.

But I also wasn't sure what Jack's expectations were now that she was back—it had been so damned much just finding out what had happened, deciding to work together to co-parent and move forward, meeting with Jack's therapist and giving him age-appropriate details.

Navigating lawyers.

Wanting my son to have a relationship with his mom, but keeping an eye on Carrie because part of me didn't trust her completely.

Lots to navigate, so I hadn't even gotten to the point in the discussion with my son about what he was expecting.

And I sure as fuck hoped it wasn't him wanting me back together with his mom.

Because that wasn't going to happen.

Because I worried if it was something he truly wanted, I wasn't going to be able to give him that. And that made me even more worried.

Because would we go back to slamming doors and *I hate yous*?

I hoped to fuck not.

"Rome," Carrie said when I got close enough to speak.

"Carrie," I replied, pausing a couple of feet away. "I didn't think we were supposed to meet with our lawyers until later this afternoon."

She rocked back slightly, lips pursing. "I wanted to talk with you before then."

"What about?"

A glance behind her then to the side, toward the double glass doors that led inside. "Can we speak somewhere more private?"

*Fuck.*

Still, in the name of familial peace, I just nodded, lifting my badge that was clipped onto one of the front pockets of my pants and swiping it at the pad by the door, listening to the lock *click* and disengage before pulling it wide for Carrie.

Bonnie was inside, tablet in her hand, moving down the hall to meet me, so we could do our typical morning debrief, discuss my schedule, and any problems (which were usually many) that had come up overnight. But when she saw me open the door for Carrie, saw my ex walk through in front of me, she paused, brows lifting, eyes sliding to mine in question.

"I'll just be a few minutes, Bon," I said. "Can you meet me in the conference room and get Danvers and Eddie on the line? I have a few things we all need to discuss."

Bonnie nodded, eyes flicking between me and Carrie. "Of course, Rome."

Then she turned away, hustling back down the hall.

"We can talk in my office, Care, yeah?"

Carrie had been staring down the hall after Bonnie, now she turned to face me. "You built all of this?"

"Yeah," I muttered, heading toward my office. "At first because I needed money to win a custody battle"—I slanted a look at her, watching her face pale as she walked beside me—"luckily, things took off and now I have two thousand employees and offices in ten countries."

Her brows lifted. "Wow."

"Yup." I pushed open my office door, waved a hand at the chairs in front of my desk. "Have a seat."

A hesitation, those brows slamming down. Then she whispered, "Thanks," and moved to one of the chairs, perching on the edge of it.

If it was anyone else, I would have sat next to them or would have leaned against the corner of my desk. I wasn't used to power plays, didn't like to sit behind my giant desk and bequeath orders to my underlings.

But...Carrie wasn't an underling, and I wasn't convinced she was here for good and—

I sat behind my desk.

"What can I do for you, Carrie?"

She didn't soften her request with any preamble. "I want my son."

My heart seized. "We're going to discuss that with the lawyers, figure out a visitation schedule."

"I want him with me."

"Carrie," I said firmly. "We can discuss that, but it's not an easy process. Jack loves you and needs you, but if I've learned anything, it's that these things take time. I think the best thing is that we work together, make it easier on everyone by coming to an agreement, so the court side of the process takes less time."

"That's not good enough," she snapped.

"You don't even have an apartment"—she was staying at a long-term hotel—"or a car"—she was renting one—"How are you going to get Jack to school? Or go to the store? What if there's an emergency and he needs to be taken to the hospital?"

"We survived four years together," she snapped. "We'll be okay."

Assurances that didn't make me feel any better.

"I'm sorry, Carrie," I said. "That's not good enough for me. I'm not going to keep you two apart, but for now, visits need to be with me or the rest of my family."

"Or with Maddie?"

The way she said Maddie's name had alarm bells blaring.

"Or with Maddie," I confirmed.

Hurt flashed through her eyes, but she didn't lose it as I half-expected. She just stared down at her hands and said, "This would all work out if you just took me back."

*Fuck.*

I bit back the curse that formed on my tongue, held in my sigh. I did, however, push up from my chair, round my desk, and crouch in front of her. "Carrie."

Her eyes came to mine.

"That's not going to happen."

She winced. "We were good once. We were great. Fucking perfect."

"And then you left."

She flinched.

"We were good," I said. "I thought you'd be my forever." I sighed. "But you left, Carrie. And you hid Jack from me and...I'm sorry, but that changed things in a way that you'll never be able to fix with me. We can find a way to get along for Jack—and God, I really want that because I love my son and I want him to have everything *he* wants. But I fought for him for four years, Care."

"I know."

"I fought to get him away from people who weren't good for him, people you exposed him to"—she flinched again—"and I'm not going to allow him to go back to that place."

"They're my family," she whispered.

"And I wanted to make one with you."

Her eyes welled with tears.

"That's not going to happen like I thought, like you thought now, coming here today. But we have a son who is great, who can use as much love as we can give him, and"—I patted her knee—"I want you to help me with that."

"I don't know if I can."

"You have to," I told her as I moved to the office door. "Your son needs you and I know you're not going to let him down."

I waited for her to get up.

To follow me to the door.

I escorted her out, watched her get in her car...

And hoped to fuck I was right.

# TWENTY-SIX

MADDIE

"What do you think of this one?"

I held up the shirt for Carrie to study.

She nodded, tapped a finger to her chin. "Yeah, I actually think that could work if we cut the sleeves off."

We were shopping.

Together.

I'd been roped into shopping—or maybe I was still making my way across to the Light Side—and part of me had loved Ro calling and asking if I wanted to join them at the local big box store to pick up pieces for Jack's costume.

He was in the school play, and his roles included both someone named Professor Rock, and a caveman, so it would require some creative costume changes.

But the moment we entered the store, Jack had dragged Ro off to go look at sports equipment.

Leaving me with Carrie.

And me wondering if things were going to be weird.

Because Ro had told me about the visit to his office.

Because they'd met with their lawyers several times over the last week, trying to figure out a custody plan.

Things were going okay.

But...I was also waiting for the other shoe to fall.

"What do you think we should do about the professor part?" I asked, because even though I was braced for the worst, I also wasn't going to be responsible for things unraveling for Jack.

Carrie tapped a finger to her chin again, something I'd noticed she did when she was considering choices. "Maybe a lab coat?"

I smiled. "That's a great idea. If he keeps it buttoned, no one will see his caveman getup until it's time for that character to make an appearance."

"I'll order one online," she said.

"Are you sure you can—?" I stopped, shook my head at myself. Stupid.

"What?" Carrie asked softly.

"I—" I sighed, decided to just level with her. "I was going to ask if you want me to order it." I waved a hand, said quietly. "In case you couldn't afford it."

A long pause, and I waited for her to snap at me. To freak out.

To say that I'd overstepped.

Carrie's hand came to mine, fingers lightly touching the back of it. "Thank you."

I looked up, held her eyes. "For what?"

Now she smiled. "I understand what they both see in you."

"What?" I whispered.

"Rome and Jack. I get it."

My heart squeezed tight, lungs frozen, words stuck inside. "Carrie."

"I thought that I could just show up and step back into my life. And then I thought I could mold the pieces of Jack and Rome's life to be what I wanted, that Rome, Jack, and I could be a happy family, could be what we *could* have been." She tucked her hair behind her ear. "But things have changed."

They *had* changed.

In Maddie's heart too.

Just this conversation—in the past I would have offered to step back, to leave Ro and Jack to Carrie. Today, I was going to work hard to find a solution that include me.

"We all love Jack," I said softly. "I think that's the most important thing."

Carrie's smile softened. "Me too." A breath. "So, now that we've gotten past the awkward and you know I'm not going to try to get between you and your man"—that had my heart pulsing...because I liked the idea of Ro being my man too much—"we can just both be here for Jack."

I studied her for a long moment, searching for any note of duplicity, any note of resentment.

But...I didn't find anything.

"And I can order the coat," she murmured. "I got my first paycheck from my new job."

My brows went up.

"It's nothing fancy. Not like yours," she added softly. "But I'm decent at serving tables and it's a good way for me to get my strength back up."

"That's really good, Carrie," I said.

A shrug. "It helps me pass my time when I'm not with Jack." A beat, that awkward making just a blip of an appearance. Because if I wasn't around, Ro might want her, and she might not need to be passing her time alone, might not want to be serving tables.

Her hand found mine again, and I glanced up.

"Don't," she said softly. "I'm..." A sigh. "I have a lot of regrets. So many. But that's not your fault. And it's not Rome's. I want you two to be happy."

"I—"

Another squeeze. "I know you don't believe me, and neither does Rome. I understand why, but...I'm working through it. I'll be better. I'll *do* better."

"Okay," I whispered.

"I'm saving up for an apartment. I know it'll take time, but I want you to know I'm trying."

"I can see that." And I could. "And I know Rome will be really happy to hear how much work you're putting in."

She nodded, opened her mouth—

"Mom! Look what Dad said I can get." Jack ran through the store, a soccer ball in his arms.

Her mouth curved and she glanced at me, eyes sparkling. "Look at my beautiful baby boy," she whispered. "How can I not give him everything I have?"

Deep inside of me, pieces shifted, slid into place.

"Show me, baby," she said, crouching down.

Ro walked up beside me, hand resting on my back, lips pressing to my temple. "Thanks for being here, cupcake."

It was such a simple statement, a small action.

But it settled in my heart, same as the rest of it did. Ro and his warm body next to mine, his arm around me. Carrie and Jack happy and chatting.

Jack showing me all of the cool features of his new soccer ball.

Going to dinner afterward and watching him turn up his nose at broccoli while Ro laughed.

Sitting at the kitchen table with him, helping him with his math homework.

Making more cupcakes, this time just for us.

Sitting in Ro's lap in his office chair, checking emails on my phone while he was on a call.

Small things.

But also the biggest ever.

Because they made me think, for the first time, that we might be able to figure this all out.

No, not *think*.

They made me *know* that I wanted this.

So much more than the fear.

"Christ, baby," Ro groaned the next week, hands going to my waist, fingers digging into my flesh.

It was late and we'd put Jack to bed together.

After cooking together.

After playing with domesticity for the last couple of weeks. Okay, not playing, but *doing.* Spending time together, not distancing myself and stepping aside.

Eating dinner. Texting. Talking on the phone. Hanging with Jack.

Not freaking out when he pulled me down into his lap at the Hutchins Family Game Night.

I hadn't even shied away from the knowing look Mel had tossed me, nor the gleeful one that Ash had sent my way.

Probably because—

I froze, straddling Ro's thighs, his cock buried deep.

He groaned again, trying to pull my hips back into motion.

But—as good as that felt—I didn't move. Not yet.

I needed to tell him something first.

"Cupcake," he warned when I just held fast.

"Honey," I murmured, leaning in, brushing my lips over his.

He didn't let it stay a brush, one hand sinking into my hair, turning the kiss hot and wet and almost making me forget what I was doing, what I wanted to tell him.

Probably because the kiss sent my hips moving, and that was...*yeah.*

It was fucking good.

It was incredible.

But...I wanted, *needed* him to know that I was—

Gathering every bit of control I could muster, I managed to stop grinding on him, to stop kissing him, to stop driving us both to the edge, and said, "I gave up my hotel room."

Now *he* froze, halting on the drive upward, the fingers that were still on my hip clenching for a second before he gentled the hold.

Because of course he did.

His other palm came to my jaw, tilting my head back so he could stare into my eyes. "You gave up your hotel room, cupcake?"

I inhaled, held it until the panic that wanted to well up faded. "Yeah, honey, I did."

His smile made any and all of the fear worth it.

"I'm coming to the Light Side," I whispered.

No. The gentleness on his face was even better.

"I'm going to—*ack!*"

I was on my back a second later, Ro on top of me. He stroked his fingers along my cheek. "*You're* not going to do anything except be you, baby." He kissed me hard and long and *wet* enough to leave my chest heaving and my mind fuzzy with desire. "*We're* going to make a beautiful life together."

"I'm—"

"Baby," he warned.

I pressed my palm to his mouth. "Shh," I murmured before I removed it. When he was silent, nodding at me to go on, I said, "*I'm* going to move in."

His eyes went on.

"Because I also told Brooks that I couldn't take the job."

"*Baby.*"

I slid my palm down, placed it over his chest, knowing more deeply than I'd ever known anything that *this* was the right decision, taking this step, making this leap, trusting Ro with my heart. "I'm ready to make that beautiful life together."

He grinned.

Then he started moving again.

And we started building our beautiful life with a beautiful...night.

# TWENTY-SEVEN

RO

"I see you finally did it."

I glanced up when Mel walked out onto the back porch. "Did what?"

She passed me a beer and leaned back against the railing, arms crossed, studying me closely in a way she never would have years ago.

But my brother and her had built something special, a framework that supported her.

Don't get me wrong, Mel was strong as fuck and had grown and pushed through a severe amount of trauma, but she'd done a lot of that growing with my brother taking her back.

Something I was determined to do with my woman, who had no little amount of her own trauma.

"You saw Maddie."

I inhaled, fingers tracing patterns on the outside of the glass bottle. "I've always seen her."

Mel smiled her gentle smile, but there was a note of chiding in her voice. "No," she said. "You've always seen what she wanted to show you. Now you see the real Maddie, see how beautiful and wonderful she is."

I wanted to argue, wanted to say that I'd always seen her, but, as usual, Mel was right.

I hadn't seen through the mask.

Not until...

"I do now," I murmured.

Mel bumped her shoulder with mine. "I know you do." A hint of tart. "Which is why I said so."

I snorted. "Did you learn your sass from Maddie?"

"Maddie is wonderful," she said. "But my sass is all self-developed."

"Damn right it is." I lifted my beer toward her and she clinked her bottle against mine.

We both drank deeply, quiet falling between us, but that wasn't unusual. Mel was quieter and soft spoken in general, much more so than the rest of us, and while I could be the life of the party, could fight with my siblings for dominion over the conversation (hello being one of eight kids with only one parent and only so much attention to go around), I appreciated the quiet.

Hence the reason I'd slipped out onto the back deck, leaving Maddie to *her* dominion.

*Nerts.*

I smiled, thinking about how she'd so easily destroyed me that last round and how much I'd loved to watch her do her victory dance.

I thought about that feeling I'd had from the first moment I'd truly looked beneath the shield.

The beauty within.

The sense of her belonging to me. To being *mine*.

The love that had begun as a small feeling and grown into something...*huge*.

"Ro?" Mel asked softly.

"I love her," I blurted.

Mel's face changed, concern morphing to amusement. "Yeah, hon. You do."

I winced. "Probably should have told her that first."

Mel shrugged. "I'm good at keeping secrets."

"Quiet, sneaky Mel," I teased.

"Maybe," she agreed. "But I also just love my family"—another nudge of her shoulder against mine—"and my friend"—a glance toward the windows, where my family and the two game tables were spot lit against the dark of the night.

"I love you, too, Mel."

She smiled up at me. "I know, hon. Now," she said. "How are you going to tell my friend you love *her?*"

"I don't know," I admitted. "But it sure as fuck is going to be special."

———

A week later and I still hadn't found a special enough way to tell the woman who was in my heart that I loved her.

We'd spent every night together—there was no sneaking from my bed, disappearing from my life and living in the shadows.

It was soccer games and kicking the ball around with Jack in the back yard.

It was me learning that I did not just throw her expensive underwear into the washer.

It was taking turns cooking dinner and discovering she had an addiction to reality television and planning videos on YouTube, even though she had never—and had no plans—to own a paper planner (see? I was even learning the terminology).

We were together. Building trust and memories and encouraging her to stay on the Light Side.

We were in the moment.

But we hadn't yet experienced what I suspected was forthcoming—

A seven-year-old having a meltdown.

It was bad timing—he'd had a nightmare and hadn't slept well, then played his final soccer game of the season this morning, followed by a team party. *Then* he'd had a friend's birthday party at a local arcade.

Interrupted sleep. Sports. Pizza and cake and soda. Running around like a crazed minion for a couple of hours before eating more pizza and cake and downing about a gallon of soda.

And now Carrie was supposed to have a couple of hours with him at her new apartment.

Not an overnight—we weren't there yet.

But introducing him to the space, getting them comfortable being together (while I hung on the couch).

Progress.

Only, I could already see this wasn't going to go well.

And although Carrie had been flexible and easygoing, adjusting to the ebb and flow of Jack over the last weeks, putting the effort in, not making things weird with me and Maddie after I'd quashed her hopes of getting back together, today she hadn't been interested in changing up their plans.

I got it.

She'd bought ingredients to bake an old family recipe—baking being something Jack was getting hooked on after making all those cupcakes with Maddie—and didn't want them to go to waste.

So, now we were walking up the stairs to Carrie's apartment, Jack bouncing along beside me.

And rubbing his eyes.

And talking a mile a minute.

And...crash imminent.

Carrie opened the door, ushered us inside, and she and Jack settled into a board game while I checked emails. I thought, for a bit as I listened to them giggle and tease each other that maybe I was wrong, that my parental instincts were off.

I was—unfortunately—proved correct about twenty minutes later.

"That's okay," Carrie was saying. "It doesn't have to be perfectly even."

"Maddie says baking is a science and we need to measure exactly."

That sounded like something Maddie *would* say.

"Well, it doesn't have to be perfectly even in *this* case."

"Yes, it does."

"I—"

"Maddie says if we're going to do something, we should do it right."

"I—"

"And Dad agrees with her."

I winced.

"And Maddie—"

I heard a sigh, something clinking down a little too hard on the counter. "Maddie doesn't know everything," Carrie said. "And neither do I or your dad. But I *do* know in this recipe that it's okay to have a little extra flour because—"

"It says one cup. I'm doing one cup—"

"Jack." A little sharp. "It's *fine*."

Something else clinked against the counter and I stood up, intending to intervene.

Only I didn't get that far.

"I'm doing one cup!" he shouted. "It says one and I'm doing one and—"

"Just stop. You don't need—"

A grunt. "Give it!"

Something fell with a *thunk* I really didn't like—because that *thunk* meant a big mess had just been made.

"You're helping clean that up."

"No, I'm not!" Jack shouted. "It's your fault. You tried to grab it from me."

"Jack," Carrie snapped.

I hurried into the kitchen, saw a mess of flour on the floor, the cabinets, all over the front of Carrie's shirt.

Yup. That was a *big* mess.

"When you participate in making messes," Carrie said, tone brittle but calm, "you need to participate in cleaning them up."

Jack's face screwed up and I knew what was coming.

Unfortunately, even though I opened my mouth, I didn't react quickly enough to stop it from happening.

"I hate you!" Jack yelled.

Shit.

"Jack," Carrie said, her hurt palpable even from across the room.

"I hate you!" He stomped his foot. "I hate you! *I hate you!*"

"Jack," I warned.

Too late. Much too fucking late. My son stopped shouting, stopped with the H word, but he shot me a tear-filled glare and ran from the room, down the hall, and...a door slammed.

Leaving me with a distraught Carrie and a giant mess—physical and emotional—to clean up.

*Christ.*

Carrie rotated slowly to face me, tears on her cheeks.

"It's okay," I told her. "I know it hurts when he says that but he doesn't really hate you."

"My baby," she whispered.

I crossed to her, pulled her into a tight hug, probably getting flour all over me, but that was the least of my concerns right then. "That fucking hurts. I know it does. He told me it enough times since he came to live with me that I know it's not easy to shrug off. But he doesn't mean it, Care. He's been through more in a few years than most people have in a lifetime, and sometimes those emotions get ahold of him. It's not right," I added. "And we should bring it up in our next therapy appointment, but it's not about you. Not really."

"No," Carrie said. "It's not about me." Her lips pressed flat and released. "It's about fucking *Maddie.*"

"Carrie," I warned.

"It's true." She pushed away from me, threw up her arms. "Isn't it great that Maddie helped Rome fight for his son? He wouldn't even be in America if it wasn't for her!" She laughed. "Isn't it great that Maddie used all of her connections to fight for an innocent child? I know my family wasn't the best, but if she hadn't stuck her nose into my life, Jack would have been there when I woke up. I wouldn't be here now, having supervised visits with my son, and hearing that Maddie does it this way so that's the only way, that Maddie knows everything, that Maddie is an all-powerful, amazing *goddess* who can do no wrong." She bent and picked up the now empty bag of flour. "Especially, when it's Maddie's fault we're not together as a family in the first place!"

I moved to her, crouching down, fixing her in place with a laser-eyed glare. "That's not true or fair, and you know it."

My tone was cold, and maybe it penetrated, or maybe she just needed to vent that shit out of her.

"And if I hear you say that around Jack, I swear to fuck, I will stop being nice, stop trying to make this fucked-up situation work." I leaned in, dropped my voice even lower. "Maddie is the best thing that's ever happened to me, and she's good for Jack. We agreed that the more people who love him, the better. So, you need to decide right here, right now to put all of your bullshit aside and remember *who* left, *who* fucked up, and *who* was the one here to help me put the pieces together."

"Rome," she whispered.

I stood, shook my head. "Pull yourself together," I growled. "I'll get Jack and we will both help you clean up the mess. Then I'm taking him home so that he can go to bed."

"I can clean—"

"Wipe your tears," I ordered, turning for the hall. "I'll be back."

I moved down the hall, got Jack to open the door, talked to him and he apologized. Then we cleaned up the spilled flour, got our shit, and went home.

He was quiet, but I figured it was because of the fight.

It wasn't until later that I would learn he'd come back after the door slammed.

That he'd been standing in the hall the whole time.

# Twenty-Eight

MADDIE

"Hey, bud," I said, reaching for Jack's backpack like I always did.

He sidestepped me. "I got it."

I lifted my brows but didn't otherwise comment. "Everything okay with school?"

"Yup. It was fine."

His tone was off, and I could feel the waves of anger rolling off him. I debated pushing this, delving into why he was upset, but figured the grassy area out front of school wasn't the ideal time or place for pushing him.

He'd been quiet since the blowup with Carrie a couple of days ago.

But I had been too.

Because Ro's ex...well, clearly, she still had a tangle of emotions about me and Ro and Jack and all of us interacting together, all of us having a role in Jack's life.

And for once in my life, I didn't know how to fix it.

Instead, I found myself holding my breath, worrying about how it would all turn out.

It would be okay.

It had to be.

Because I'd finally taken a leap and Ro had caught me, and I'd never felt safer or more seen or more...loved.

Even just thinking it had my heart picking up speed, little flutters gathering in my belly.

I had the big, beautiful family I'd always craved.

And I wasn't standing on the sidelines, watching from afar while I buzzed around and tried to ensure everything was perfect for everyone else and sacrificing myself in the process. I was fully in the mix—and yeah, it was dizzying, not being able to pull back and just problem solve, to be living in the messy reality of the Hutchinses.

But it was also beautiful.

So, I didn't fight Jack over taking his backpack and I didn't press on school. Instead, I employed one of my go-to tactics to get people to talk...and if they didn't, still had delicious, carby side benefits. "Want to go to Molly's?"

A shrug. "Sure."

Not exactly the excited response I'd expected.

But it wasn't in the negative and life wasn't always full of bouncy, enthusiastic moments.

I could take a *sure.*

We drove to Molly's and he was still quiet. We walked inside, ordered, and sat at a table. And he was still quiet.

We sat for a bit, waiting for our treats, and though I tried to engage him in conversation...he was still quiet.

"Thanks for the cookie, Maddie," he said, after we'd eaten in—no surprise—quiet, and driven home (yup, Ro's place was now my home and that felt fucking *great*) *in quiet,* and walked into our house in...*quiet.*

I was so relieved to actually hear his voice and not have it be in response to one of the copious questions I'd been tossing his way, trying to engage him in conversation that I just ruffled his hair. "Anytime, bud. Need help with your homework?"

He shook his head. "No, I'm going to practice." He had a goal in the back yard, a net behind it to stop his newly purchased soccer ball from escaping into the neighbor's lawn.

"Then homework?"

A nod as he dumped his backpack on the counter and headed out into the yard.

I spent the next few minutes unpacking the stuff that always made it inside—leaves and sticks and random papers that were always crunched up at the bottom. I rinsed out his lunchbox and left it on the counter so Ro and Jack could make his lunch—they'd gotten into the habit of putting together fancy charcuterie-type meals after Jack had seen a video on YouTube.

Then I returned some phone calls—I was neck deep in preparation for the distribution center outside of Omaha—did some emails and debated between starting dinner and ordering something in since I really didn't feel like cooking.

Ro would be home soon—he could make that call.

Which would probably be to take one look at my face, realize I didn't feel like cooking, and order food in for us.

Because he saw me and protected me and—

"Is it true?"

I turned and glanced over my shoulder, saw that Jack had come back in while I'd been putzing around. "Is what true?"

He clutched the ball to his chest, hovering in the doorway of the kitchen as though he was ready at any moment to bolt down the hall, as though if I answered this wrong, the entire world might fall apart.

"Did you break up my family?"

I was expecting trouble with school, conflicted feelings about a friend. Frustration about soccer or a recipe he wanted to try.

I wasn't expecting *that*.

"I don't understand, bud. I wasn't with your dad until recently, and didn't even know him until you were already born—"

"But you broke us up. Ruined my family," he said, fingers digging into his ball. "I heard my mom say that. I-I—" He lifted his chin. "I *heard* them talking about it."

Presumably Rome and Carrie.

And that fight from the other day.

That Jack had heard.

*Fuck.*

I lifted my hand, rubbed at the headache forming there. "It's complicated, bud. You know that your mom was sick, right?"

He nodded.

"And that everyone thought that she was de—er, *gone.*"

His bottom lip wobbled, but he nodded again. And God, I just wanted to cross to him, to take him in my arms. But when I took a step in his direction, intending to do just that, he backed up, increasing the distance between us, little fingers clenching that ball tighter.

"And the people you were staying with, do you remember?"

Another nod.

"Well, they weren't looking after you like they should have, so when your dad found out about you, he knew he needed to get you here, to make sure you were safe, that you had a family who would love you and keep you safe and—"

His eyes flashed. "You helped him."

"I—" I didn't like his tone, how it was flat and cold. I didn't like how it made the knot of fear tighten in my belly. "Yes, bud. It's not a secret that I did everything to help your dad get you here. I knew some people who were able to assist when things got tricky for your dad and I got them involved."

He looked away, shoulders hunching then looked back, the anger on his face icy cold. "So, you *did* ruin my family."

That was worse. A punch to the gut, so hard I nearly bent over from the surprisingly rough jab.

"No," I said. "That's not—"

"If you hadn't helped, I would be in Australia and my mom would have her house and she wouldn't be sad anymore."

"Jack," I began.

"It's *your* fault she's sad. It's your fault she cried."

I sucked in a breath, released it slowly. "No, bud. She's sad because it's a sad situation and she cries sometimes because she missed out on a lot. And she cried the other day because *you* used unkind words with her and told her you hated her, just like you've said that to your dad a *lot* of times."

He paled, inched back.

But I needed him to get this, to understand, to stop hurting the people he loved.

I focused on what *I* needed him to do.

Not on what he needed from *me*.

Later, I would realize I'd overstepped, that I wasn't the parent, that I shouldn't have gone so far.

But right then?

I was in too deep.

"Words hurt, honey, and those words *especially* hurt your mom and dad. More so after everything all of you have been through." I moved then, not stopping as he slid back, just increasing my speed so I caught up with him at the bottom of the stairs, crouching in front of him so we were at eye level. "You have a lot of people in your life who love you and want the best for you, and you need to be more careful with them."

The soccer ball dropped from his hands, bouncing off my leg and rolling across the hall, through the passthrough, and into the kitchen.

"You're an awesome kid—"

He whirled around.

"And I know you can do better."

He started running up the stairs.

"Because we all love you *so* much."

He reached the top of the stairs and glanced back, tears on his cheeks.

But then he was spinning back around, sprinting down the hall.

His door slammed.

I sighed, rose to my feet, and moved into the kitchen.

I'd make dinner after all, give him some time to cool down so we could talk it through.

So...I did just that—got ingredients together and set them out on the counter, started chopping and getting everything going on the stove before I turned on the oven. Answering a work call as I sautéed onions. Cleaning out his soccer cleats so they'd be ready for the next time he played. Picking up the soccer ball from where it had rolled into the corner, setting it on the kitchen island.

I'd bring it up to him later.

After I gave him that time.

I flitted around until there were no more emails to answer and dinner was simmering on the stove and the bread was ready to go in the oven.

Then I braced myself for a difficult conversation.

Only, it was then that I realized...

The soccer ball was no longer on the island.

Heart twisting, I pushed off the stool, closing my laptop, and heading out of the kitchen. The worry that had been in the back of my mind burst forth, jolting me into action when I saw his jacket wasn't on the row of hooks on the wall, when his backpack was no longer sitting below it like I had left it after cleaning it out earlier.

"Shit," I whispered and hauled ass up the stairs.

Ran down the hall to Jack's room.

Threw open the door...

It was empty.

# Twenty-Nine

Ro

I was in a great fucking mood.

The compliance issue from weeks back had finally—officially—been laid to rest, and I was going to thank my woman in the best possible way that night.

Several times even.

Grinning, I hit the clicker, wondered if Ash and Mel and the kids might want to take Jack for a super special sleepover. Something that would then free up the house so I could fuck Maddie on the kitchen counter and the stairs and my office again and not have to listen with half an ear for my son. Worrying that he might hear us, come down to investigate and...then be scarred for life.

I loved my son.

I just...it was time to tell Maddie exactly what she meant to me.

Because I'd figured it out. There was nothing I could do—no grand gesture, no amount of flowers or fancy dinners or new email management program I could purchase for her that would be better than me just taking her in my arms and telling her how much I loved her.

The others were great, thoughtful even.

They just weren't what Maddie needed.

I pulled out my cell, called my brother, and he promised to swing by on the way home from his office to snag Jack.

So, I would be winning in two ways.

Making my kid happy.

Getting Maddie to herself and completing her ascension to the Light Side.

I cut the engine, grabbed my messenger bag and cell and got out of my car, moving into the house at light speed.

Wanting to see my kid and my Maddie.

*Needing* to see them both.

The moment I hit the mudroom, a delicious scent hit my nose, and I knew that I was going to thank my woman an extra time for whatever mouthwatering meal she had made for Jack and me. But first I had to find her.

Chuckling, I toed off my shoes, moved down the short hall and into the kitchen, expecting to see Maddie where she usually was, sitting on a stool, laptop open, Jack next to her (or in the back yard, kicking his ball around)—

But the space was empty.

Frowning, I moved into the living room.

Maybe they'd put on one of their favorite YouTubers? Or a Gold game, since my son had recently decided that hockey was the second-best sport ever.

But that was empty too.

A *thunk* sounded upstairs, and I frowned, moving out into the hall, bounding up the steps. Maybe they were playing a board game in Jack's room or—

Another *thunk*.

This one louder, like a door had been opened and firmly closed.

But not like Jack usually did it.

That was a full-on slam that reverberated through the house.

Maybe they were playing...hide and seek?

"Jack!"

Only *that* wasn't Maddie calling my son's name with humor or exasperation because he was really good at hide and seek (which he was). That was...panic.

And it had me moving faster, bursting into Jack's room and seeing...

Maddie with tears pouring down her cheeks, mascara streaked beneath each eye. She whirled around when I came in, hope on her face for a heartbeat before it disintegrated. Then she was rushing over to me.

"Ro. Oh God. *Rome.*" She collided with my body and I caught her so she didn't bounce off and hit the carpet.

"What happened?" I asked, my insides in absolute turmoil.

"I—" She sucked in a hitching breath, released it in a hiss. "When I picked up Jack from school, he seemed a little off and quiet, like he's been the last couple of days."

Something I'd noticed too.

I'd just figured he was recovering from the big weekend. Though, we had a therapy appointment scheduled in the next couple of days.

"Yeah, cupcake, I know," I prompted when she closed her eyes, nails digging into my chest. "What happened?"

"I took him to Molly's for some treats, hoping he'd open up, but knowing that even if he didn't, that it would make him feel better because it's Molly's."

I felt my lips tip up, even though there wasn't anything amusing about this situation at all.

"And then we came home and he went out back to play and I was doing some work and—"

She sucked in another shuddering breath as I fought for patience, knew that she would give me the rest of it.

"Then he asked me if it was true."

Fuck, I really didn't like the sound of that. "Asked if *what* was true?"

"If I'd broken up his family."

*"Fuck,"* he whispered.

"I know. I can't lie and say it didn't hurt, but then he started talking about if I wasn't here, you and him and Carrie would be in Australia and Carrie wouldn't be sad anymore. How it was my fault that she was crying the other night and then—"

She closed her eyes, shook her head.

"What?" I rasped.

"I told him Carrie wasn't sad because of me. That the *situation* was sad and she wished she hadn't missed out on so much time with him."

Okay, that didn't seem bad.

"But then"—her eyes came back to mine—"I think I messed up."

I inhaled, but she went on before I could say anything.

"I told him his mom was sad because he told her he hated her and that she cried because he used unkind words, and that when he says that to you, it hurts you too."

My throat went tight.

"I, um, I think I should have let you or Carrie handle it, but Jack and I are close and I wanted him to know that those words hurt people and hurt you a lot and that he should be thankful for everyone in his life who loves him."

"Then what?" I rasped.

"I—" She nibbled at her bottom lip. "He stormed off, and I gave him some space, but then when I took a break from emails and cooking dinner and—" Another breath. "I looked up and saw that his soccer ball wasn't on the counter anymore. And his backpack wasn't in the hall. And his jacket—"

My heart seized.

"It's not on the hook."

"What the fuck did you do?" I whispered.

She turned around. "I thought he might be hiding from me or back in the yard, but I didn't find him in here or out there and his stuff is gone, and I don't know. I thought he *had* to be in here." She swept toward the closet, pulled it open, started shoving stuff to the side. "He's *got* to be here." Finding nothing, she straightened, move to the bed, where there was a little storage compartment beneath, something that happened to be Jack-sized, so he ended up chilling in it with his tablet frequently.

But that was empty too.

"What the fuck did you do?"

She turned to me, face pale, makeup a mess.

"Maybe the bathroom," she whispered, tugging open the door to the en suite.

Revealing it was empty.

"Your office," she said quickly, starting to move by me.

I caught her. "What *the fuck* did you do?"

"I—" She shook her head, was trembling as she pulled out of my hold, as she ran down the stairs, as I followed her, as we both pushed into my office.

Which was empty too.

And...I lost it.

"*What the fuck did you do?!*"

# Thirty

Tears were still pouring down my cheeks, but I didn't even feel the constant flow of them.

Probably because I was no longer sobbing.

I'd finished with that after Ro had bellowed at me and then turned away, running through the house, much like I had been doing when he'd come home, searching every nook and cranny, trying not to believe what had to have happened actually happened.

But probably understanding it had with each moment that passed.

The truth sinking in like a foxtail poking into the skin, burrowing in, ruining the flesh beneath as it dug a painful path through the tissue.

Jack's words.

Ro's words.

They'd burrowed deep.

They'd cut the ropes, sending one side of my bridge cascading down into the ravine, shaking me loose just when I'd lifted a foot to step off onto the Light Side.

I was tumbling down into the darkness below.

Knowing that the collision with the ground was going to *hurt*.

Now I wiped my cheeks and called Ash and Mel as Ro continued to search, moving to the back yard.

The call helped center me, helped me pull it together with a task, with a mental to do list of everything that I needed to do.

Call the family, make sure that Jack wasn't with them.

Enlist them in the search.

Call Carrie. Do the same.

Call the po-police.

That had my eyes welling again, especially when Ash said that Jack wasn't with him but he was already on his way because Rome had arranged a sleepover at his place so Ro and I could celebrate.

Celebrate what, I didn't know.

And *wouldn't* now.

I hung up with Ash, swiped a finger beneath each eye, and then dialed Mel, filling her in, discovering that Jack wasn't there either, asking her to call one-half of the Hutchinses while I took care of Carrie and the other half.

Phone calls that yielded nothing—or well, didn't yield what I so desperately wanted: Jack safe and secure and with them.

But Jack hadn't shown at any of their houses.

So, the only thing the calls yielded were more people heading here to join in with the search.

"I'm going to look at the park."

Terse words that had me looking up from my phone, from the map I'd pulled up and the search grid I'd been mentally erecting. "Okay," I whispered, knowing he was worried, but almost desperate that he stop, draw me into his arms, and apologize for yelling, for all but telling me it was my fault.

We didn't have time for that.

We needed to find Jack.

But, still, when he turned away without his expression softening, without him telling me that he didn't mean it, I felt something inside me crack.

No, *shatter*. The pieces falling down to my feet, slicing as they dropped.

He turned back.

Those pieces flew up, ready to be repaired.

"Call Blake," he said tersely. "Fill him in and see what he suggests."

"Okay," I whispered again.

He nodded, stalked down the hall, disappearing into the kitchen. I heard the door to the garage slam, his engine start up.

And sniffed.

Realized that dinner was burning on the stove.

I hurried over to it, flicked off the gas, shoved the scorched pan into the sink, and cranked on the water.

I was crying again.

But I still called Blake.

———

"Here you go," I murmured softly to Wyatt and Jeremy as they took the papers I'd printed off for the search grid.

Using cinnamon—the password Ro had given me, not the spice—to get into his computer.

My heart pulsed, but I shoved it down.

It had been at least an hour since I noticed Jack was missing, and I'd spent the first twenty running around, being an idiot, the next five being berated, and the last thirty-odd since pulling my shit together and doing something productive.

I was going to fix this.

I *had* too.

"We'll call you if we find anything," Jer said softly.

"Okay," I whispered.

They turned and left, and I went back to the phone, back to the search grids.

Back to burying my hurt by fixing things.

Only, I didn't know how to fix *this*. What if something terrible had happened to Jack? What if he was out there with some creep, scared and hurt and—

There was a knock at the front door.

I dropped my phone on the counter, grabbed yet another map I'd printed out, and ran over to answer it, fully prepared to send another of Ro's siblings or their spouses or friends off onto another search pattern.

I wasn't prepared to open the door and see...

Jack.

Standing there with his backpack on his shoulders and his jacket on and his soccer ball in his arms.

"Oh my God." I reached forward, wrapped my arms around him, and hugged him tight. "*Oh my God.*" I was crying again, but there was no helping it. I was just so glad he was here and safe and *here*. So, I held him close, gave into the moment.

But only for a second.

Then I managed to pull myself away from Jack long enough to drag him inside, to slam and lock the door, and then tow him along with me into the kitchen, snatch up my cell, and call Ro.

"What?" he answered on the first ring.

"J-jack's h-here," I stammered out.

"Where?"

"Here at the house."

"I'll be there in five." He clicked off.

I sucked in a breath, spun back to face Jack, half-convinced he'd have disappeared again.

But he was still standing there.

Only, his face was stark as he came over to me and slipped his hand into mine. "Now I made *you* cry," he whispered.

"No, honey," I said quickly. "This was my fault. I was scared and—"

His arms wrapped around me, squeezed me tight. "I'm sorry," he whispered.

"I'm sorry too."

We held each other until the door to the garage slammed open, Ro running inside, sweeping toward us. Jack stepped out of my hold, and Ro swept him up in one smooth movement.

Jack started crying.

Ro buried his head in Jack's neck, shoulders shaking.

I slipped away, gave them that moment.

Taking the opportunity to activate the Hutchins phone tree.

And then, when Ro and Jack moved into the back yard, and I saw them sitting on the deck stairs, staring out at the landscaping, heads bent and serious conversation underway, I took another opportunity.

To pack a bag.

To slip out through the front door.

To get in my car and drive away.

Then...

To make one more phone call.

"Brooks," I said when the man on the other end picked up. "Do you still want me to take that job?"

# Thirty-One

Ro

I didn't know where to start.

How *did* one start to encapsulate the last couple of hours to a seven-year-old?

I wanted to throttle him and just drag him close again and hug him for a century. I wanted to call his therapist for an emergency appointment so we could fix it and this would never happen again. I wanted to yell and terrify him so much that he wouldn't so much as dare.

I wanted to tell him how scared I was and how much I loved him and—

"Do you hate *me* now?" he asked quietly.

My heart rolled over in my chest. "No, bud, I could never hate you."

"No matter what?"

"No matter what."

"But"—he bent, tugged at the hem of his shorts, fussing with the fabric, clearly scared to say whatever he was going to say next— "I said I hated you a lot."

"I know," I said quietly. "And I can't lie, bud, that hurt my feelings a whole lot."

Jack's shoulders hunched.

"But I know that you've been through a lot and have a ton of big emotions. I get why those feelings would come out sometimes." I looked at him, watched his frame grow even stiffer. "That's why we shouldn't use those words."

Quiet.

For long enough that I wondered if I should have let him off the hook.

Like I'd said, he'd been through a lot and tonight was no exception and—

"I'm sorry."

I wanted to say it was okay, but, of course, it wasn't. So, I settled for putting my arm around him and tugging him into my side. "Thank you for apologizing."

"I won't say it again."

"I believe you," I said. "And—" I leaned back enough to look him square in the eyes. "And you won't run away from home again, right?"

He'd started to nod, but that had him freezing, frowning. "I didn't run away."

I lifted my brows in question.

"Mrs. Donovan"—his teacher—"said that sometimes I should just take a walk if I'm upset. That way I don't get into fights at school anymore." He shrugged. "I was mad—*really* mad—so I decided to take a walk."

"You took your backpack and jacket, bud."

"Maddie says it's been getting cold, so it's always good to have one. And I needed something to hold my soccer ball."

"I—" I clamped my lips together, trying to find fault with any of that.

I couldn't. Minus—

"Next time you take a walk, you need to keep it to our neighborhood, bring your phone, and tell me, your mom, Maddie, or another responsible adult before you leave."

His eyes went wide. "Okay."

"Now," I said. "That's out of the way, so I think we need to discuss what made you so mad in the first place."

Jack's eyes went wider, his cheeks turning pink.

"Maddie had nothing to do with my and your mom's relationship. Your mom and I ended for a number of reasons and they don't have anything to do with you either, or living here or in Australia."

"What'd they have to do with then?"

"That's not really any of your business, bud. Maybe it's something that we can talk about when you get older, when you have your own significant other. But right now," I added. "All you need to know is that sometimes people grow apart and relationships don't work, and none—*none*—of that is your fault."

He was silent for a long moment, staring off into the landscaping. Then he looked up at me, said simply, "Okay."

I drew him into my side again. "And you need to know that I love you, no matter what."

"Okay," said a little quieter, a little wetter. Like he was a few seconds away from crying. "I'm sorry," he whispered.

"I know."

He sniffed.

I held him close.

And when I sensed that he'd settled, that he was ready, I drew us up to our feet. "Let's find Maddie and order something in for dinner, yeah?"

I'd seen the remnants of whatever had once smelled delicious in the sink, the pan blackened, smelled the tinge of smoke in the air from the ruined meal, knew that whatever hard work Maddie had put into it had been for naught.

"Can I go take a shower?"

I almost laughed. Trying to get Jack into the shower on a

normal day was a supremely difficult task. That my kid had offered of his own volition boded good things. "Sure, bud," I said, ruffling his hair. "I'll find Maddie and we'll sort out dinner, yeah?"

"Yeah." He turned for the stairs, started up them, and I found myself watching, the panic and worry gone, but the ache I had in my chest was still there.

Because, goddamn, had it been an evening.

I exhaled, started to turn away.

But the sound of pounding footsteps had me halting, had me bracing, Jack launching himself at me. I caught him, was nearly brought to tears by the tight hug. *Was* brought to tears when he squeezed me one more time then murmured, "I love you, Dad."

Then he was off again, running up the stairs, disappearing down the hall, leaving me there with a tight throat and a tear dripping down my cheek.

I rubbed it away, exhaled, and turned for the kitchen, walking through the passthrough. "Cupcake, you would not believe—"

I froze, saw the space was empty.

Frowning, I moved down the hall, looked in my office, found it empty as well.

And considering this felt far too much like what I'd experienced earlier when searching for Jack, I decided to expedite the process and just call her.

It went straight to voicemail.

I called again.

More voicemail.

"Christ," I muttered, moving to the kitchen and out to the garage. Maybe she'd gone out, wanted to give Jack and I space. But there wasn't a note on the board, telling me that. And when I called a third time, it still went to voicemail.

And *that* was when my stomach began to sink.

She always took my calls.

From the moment she'd taken that leap with me, she'd *always* picked up.

I shot a text off as I went into our bedroom...

And that was when I saw it—

The drawer that was slightly ajar in the closet, her clothes missing from the hangers. Stomach sinking, I moved into the bathroom, saw that her makeup was gone, her toothbrush.

Her lotion from the bedside table.

Her book that had been beside it.

Hands shaking, I called her again.

Voicemail.

"*Fuck.*"

I called Ash.

But he didn't pick up either.

Mel did, though, and her voice was harsher than I'd ever heard it before when she asked me, "What the fuck do you think you are doing?"

# THIRTY-TWO

MADDIE

I had to give Brooks credit.

The man moved quickly.

I guess that was what happened when a person was a billionaire.

There was a jet waiting on the tarmac by the time I got out of my car.

And attendants.

Who opened my door.

"I—"

"Mr. Saxton"—Brooks—"told us to arrange for storage for your vehicle," the well-dressed brown-haired man said, extending a hand to help me out of the car.

"But—"

He bent across me, pushed the button to undo my belt. "I can assure you your vehicle will be perfectly safe."

"I—"

He tugged, and I found myself out of my car. "Is your bag in the trunk?" he asked.

"I—" But he'd already released my hand and moved to the trunk, and, yup, he was removing my suitcase, wheeling it toward the plane.

I followed...because what else could I do?

Forget about my makeup and my favorite pair of heels and launch myself into the car? Go back to Ro, to Jack?

My heart convulsed.

I didn't want to leave them.

But...*no.* I couldn't go back. Not after how he'd looked at me. Not after he'd shouted at me. Not after he'd *blamed* me.

After they'd *both* blamed me.

"Ms. Ronaldo?"

I blinked, realized I was staring off into space, realized that someone had driven my car off, realized that the man who'd retrieved my luggage was waiting for me to precede him up the jet's stairs.

There was only one way to go.

It was to crawl back to the Dark Side, to keep myself safe and secure...and that started with taking the job Brooks had offered. Finding some distance, rebuilding my walls. Staying on the outside.

Where I belonged.

I hurried across the tarmac, moving toward the man and my suitcase and the stairs. Then I took a deep breath and ascended.

To my future.

To what I deserved.

To—

No. I deserved better. I deserved to have good things. I deserved a man who would take my back like he'd promised. I deserved...to be happy.

And I wasn't.

But was it because of what Ro said, and how he said it, and... how I'd responded.

Collapsing.

Turning inward.

Sliding down into the abyss.

Not standing up for myself.

Didn't I at least deserve that much?

No—*yes!* I fucking did.

"Have a seat anywhere you'd like Ms. Ronaldo." I'd reached the top of the stairs, realized one of the flight attendants was staring at me.

I hurried over to one of the plush leather seats, buckled in, and tried to navigate my way through the tornado in my mind.

Make myself small. Run until they forgot they hated me, that they were mad at me, that they couldn't possibly love me.

Or stand up, go back, demand that *he* cut the bullshit.

That I understood it was an extreme situation but that he never talked to me like that again.

Not *fucking* ever.

I was...distraught and broken and hurt and so fucking in love with the man who fumbled the catch he'd promised to always make and—

Why did I need someone to catch me at all?

I sighed and dropped my elbows onto my knees, settled my head into my heads. God, I was such a mess and—one hundred percent—I was desperate to just run away and not face the bullshit my heart was telling me I had to sift through.

Run and hide was winning out.

Exhaling sharply, I straightened. I could do this. I could survive.

I always did.

I—

A shadow appeared in the doorway and I expected it to be the man with my luggage or the pilot or another one of the flight attendants.

Instead...Ro walked through the door.

My heart seized in my chest, so hard that I felt as though I was going to pass out. But then it seemed to kickstart, to settle, to allow air into my lungs and my mind to somewhat clear—or to clear enough for me to *feel.*

And I was feeling. Big, huge feelings—and the biggest one was that I was angry.

Really, *really* angry.

And hurt and...in love and hurt because I *was* in love. And confused and scared and—

*Angry.*

"Maddie," Ro said, striding over to me, his eyes sparking with fury as he drew close. "What the fuck are you doing?"

I started to stand, realized I was buckled in when I got stuck halfway up. I yanked at the lever, freed myself, and stood up, marching over to him, some of that anger flying free. "What am I doing?" I jabbed a finger into his chest. "What the fuck am *I* doing?"

He caught my hand. "Don't."

I tried to yank it back, but he held it fast.

"Don't, baby—"

"Don't tell me what to do!"

He rocked back slightly on his heels, shock ricocheting across his face. Whether it was because of what I said or how I'd said—cough, *yelled* it—I didn't know.

And I was too far gone to care.

"You've given me enough orders about how to act and what to fight for and what to *feel.*"

"That's not fair."

It wasn't, so I took a breath, said softly, "No, it's not. But you spun me a fantasy. You got me to trust you. You promised me the freaking world"—my voice dropped—"and then you turned on me." My anger was growing again, my tone going sharp and harsh. "You turned on me and you were mean and you yelled at me about what happened with Jack and that *wasn't my fucking fault!*"

"No," he said, moving into me, pressing our bodies together from chest to thighs. "It wasn't you, wasn't your fault, baby."

My chin came up. "And I didn't deserve to be yelled at."

His fingers stroked through my hair. "No, you didn't."

His agreement took some of the wind out of my sails, leaving me floundering, leaving me wondering what the hell I should say next.

My gaze drifted away, slid to the side, catching on those plush leather seats, confusion stealing my rage.

Because I loved him, and I was hurt.

I wanted to stay, and I *needed* to run.

"Baby."

I looked back in time to see his hand drifting toward my face, and a shiver coursed through me when he touched my cheek, cupped my jaw, tilted my head back enough to stare deeply into my eyes.

"I'm sorry," he said.

My toes curled into my shoes, digging in hard enough to make the soles of my feet cramp.

Relief and pain.

Wanting so badly to step back into the circle of his embrace.

Needing so badly to step away.

"But, baby," he murmured, drawing me back to the present. "People fight. People get mad."

My heart squeezed hard then started pounding.

"People fuck up and apologize and figure their shit out, and I *fucked up*. It was a heavy, scary situation and I didn't react how I should have. My son—fuck, I thought I'd lost him again and it wasn't your fault. It wasn't even Jack's fault. He took a walk to clear his head because they encouraged him to do that at school."

I shook my head, anger inching away.

"I told him he has to tell one of us"—my heart squeezed again —"before he does that, but he was more worried that you would be mad at him than if he'd get in trouble."

Rage transforming into...something else I didn't want to think about.

Yearning.

Forgiveness.

Worry.

For Jack. For...Ro.

I opened my mouth, to say something, *anything*, even if I didn't know what the fuck it would be, but the words didn't so much as hit my tongue because Ro tilted my head back and kissed me long enough to leave my head spinning.

Even more than it had been before.

And then—

"I love you."

# THIRTY-THREE

RO

She gasped, eyes going wide, lips parting.

Mouth so goddamned tempting that I almost bent and kissed her again.

And maybe I should have, maybe if I'd done that right in this moment, had just allowed our passion to overrule our minds, everything would have turned out differently.

But I didn't.

Because I knew that I owed her an explanation.

"I *love* you, cupcake," I said. "And I know I'm going to fuck up again and I'm going to hurt you and I'm not going to want that" —I touched her cheek—"I know I'm going to hate that it happens —I *already* hate it—but it's *gonna* happen, baby. Because people aren't perfect. Because I'm so fucking far from that it's not even funny."

Her eyes slid closed, tears gathering the corners, spilling over. "I know," she whispered. "I know that."

"I'm going to mess up and so are you." I leaned in, kissed her forehead, relief when she didn't tense or pull back fueling my words. "But if both of us don't fight for this, for *us* then we can't move forward." I slid my hand into her hair, drew her close to me. "I need you to fight for us, need you to not run when shit gets real, when it gets intense. I need to trust that beneath any disagreement or anger or fuck-up is *love*. And to trust *that* will guide us forward."

She released a shaky breath.

"I love you, and I'm sorry I hurt you. I'm sorry I stumbled fucking big time at the first hurdle we experienced, sorry I even insinuated that it was your fault when it wasn't. But, baby, it's just that, just a hurdle." I tucked her hair behind her ear. "We can get over it, move past it. We can prepare for the next one."

"What if I can't do that?" she asked quietly, eyes wide, her pulse fluttering like a hummingbird at the base of her throat, rapid flickers that belied how scared she was.

Because *I'd* put that fear into her.

And, fuck, that didn't feel good.

"You can do it," I whispered. "You're the strongest, the best woman I know."

Those eyes closed again, and she shook her head.

I ran my knuckles over her cheek, waited for them to open. "I love you."

Hope flared in pretty blue eyes. Hope that was quickly doused with bleakness. "It isn't supposed to be this hard."

"Anything really worth it is hard."

She inhaled.

"It's a battle, a struggle, and I know it will be worth it in the end."

"How do you know that?" she asked softly.

"Because you're you. Because I love the woman you are on the inside. Because you love my son and make him laugh. Because you're amazingly organized and capable and beautiful in here"—I gently tapped her temple—"and here"—the spot over her heart.

"Because you aligned yourself with a vulnerable little boy and you trusted your heart to me."

"And I got hurt," she whispered.

"Yeah, baby, you did. And I'm sorry." I cupped her jaw again. "But I'm here. I'm here to pick up the pieces and make it better. Because you deserve that and so much more. Because I know you would do the same for me."

She nibbled at the corner of her mouth.

I gently freed that bit of flesh, ran my thumb along her bottom lip. "If you want to go, *really* want to go, I won't clip your wings, cupcake. I'll stand back, let you live your life." God, that would kill, but I would find a way to do it. "Except, I think you already feel it here." I touched her chest above her heart again, felt that organ still pounding inside her rib cage. "I think you already know that if you go, you'll be leaving your family behind."

Her exhale was shaky. "Ro," she whispered.

I dropped my hand. "Think about what I said, what we have together." Then I bent in, pressed my lips to hers, kissed her gently. Slowly, softly, *forever.* "Think about the beauty we can build together if we get past this."

And then—even though it was the hardest thing I'd ever done —I turned away from the woman I loved, walked off the plane, down the stairs, gave her the time and space to process.

I gave it knowing that, any second, she would be flying down the stairs, sprinting over to me, throwing herself into my arms, telling me that this was a fucked-up situation but things would be okay, that we could work it out.

Telling me she loved me too.

So, I waited by my car.

Waited *knowing* that she was going to come out.

That we were going to get through this.

That she was going to fight for me.

For *us.*

I stood on that tarmac, and I waited.

And waited.

And fucking *waited*.

Waited as the steps were folded up and the plane door shut—knowing they would open back up, that she would run down, apology on her tongue as she came to me.

Her love for me on her tongue.

I waited as the engines roared to life.

I waited as the plane began to inch forward.

I waited knowing it was going to stop, those stairs would extend again, and *then* she would come for me, hating that she'd worried me, hating that she'd taken so long to summon her courage.

I waited as the plane increased in velocity, as it taxied down to the runway.

As it picked up speed and...elevation.

As it took off into the sky, growing smaller and smaller by the second.

Until it disappeared.

And the woman I loved had left me.

Again.

# THIRTY-FOUR

## MADDIE

I cried most of the twelve-hour flight.

And slept the rest of it.

Because it was easier to do that than accidentally make eye contact with the flight attendants and see the pity in their eyes.

The disappointment.

In me for not letting them experience a fairy tale?

For me for not allowing myself to have that happily ever after?

Maybe both. *Probably* both.

But now we'd descended and the plane door was open, and I needed to get into the car, go to the hotel. Sleep. Wake up. *Work.*

The only things that made sense.

"Your bag is waiting at the bottom of the stairs, Ms. Ronaldo."

"Okay," I rasped, throat on fire, eyes swollen and aching. "Thank you."

A nod, pity in her eyes, and then the flight attendant was turning away, going about her business, probably more than ready to be off the plane and away from the crazy, sobbing woman.

Exhaling, I ducked out through the door, made my way down

the steps and toward the black sedan waiting for me, another atten-dant—my handsome, brown-haired man from San Francisco—wheeling my bag, stowing it in the trunk. "Thank you," I murmured again when he opened the door so I could climb into the back. I started to sit on the leather seat.

Then froze, my butt several inches above the leather.

"Oh God," I whispered. "*Oh God.*"

Ro had poured out his heart to me, had told me that he loved me...and I'd walked away.

*Flown* away.

And I'd done it while *loving* him.

While knowing how hurt he'd been after Carrie had done the same.

While hearing his apology, hearing how sincere it was.

While he'd made so much sense that it should have penetrated.

And I'd gotten on a fucking plane and flown away, leaving him —and Jack—behind.

"Fuck," I whispered, still hovering above the seat. "I really fucked up."

"Yeah, you did."

I blinked, glanced up at my brown-haired attendant. "I *really* fucked up," I blurted again.

He nodded, said again, "Yeah, you did."

"I need to get home."

Another nod, and he pulled his phone out. "I'll call Mr. Saxton for another crew. You sit there and call your man and tell him that you fucked up."

Since that made a lot more sense than the bullshit swirling in my mind, I just followed instructions, sitting down, getting my cell out, powering it up, seeing dozens of missed calls, a shit-ton of texts, but ignoring them all in favor of dialing Ro.

My call went straight to voicemail.

"Shit," I whispered, trying a few more times and getting the same response.

"Mr. Saxton for you," the attendant murmured, holding out his cell.

Shit.

I'd really fucked up. And...I couldn't take the job. Again.

"Hello, Brooks?"

"Ms. Maddie." Chiding in Brooks's tone.

"I'm sorry," I whispered. "I thought it was best that I left and started over, but I can't do this, I can't leave everything and everyone I love behind, and come work for you."

Silence, long and tense enough to make me fidgety. "No, Maddie," he eventually said. "Leaving the people you love so you can start over is never the right thing to do."

My toes curled into my shoes again, sending my feet cramping.

But it was nothing compared to the pain in his words.

*That* took my breath away.

"Brooks," I began.

"There will be a new crew at the airport within the hour," he said brusquely, moving the conversation along before I could do something stupid like ask him about his heartbreak. Thank God. I didn't need to piss off Brooks Saxton. I had enough problems on my plate to deal with—and, as everyone knew, *that* was saying something.

"Thanks—"

"In the meantime," he advised. "I'd figure out how you're going to grovel."

"I—" An exhale. "I'll do that."

"See that you do."

Another breath. "Thanks Brooks. I owe you one." A shake of my head. "Or two, really."

"*Three*, Maddie." A beat. "By my count, you owe me three."

Taking the job.

Backing out.

Taking the job again.

A flight on short notice.

Backing out. Again.

Another flight on short notice.

That was six.

I didn't mention that, considering that owing Brooks Saxton three favors was already a big deal. Six would probably kill me.

"Three," I agreed and hung up, passing the phone back.

"Hang tight," the attendant said. "I'm going to help get the plane ready for your return to your sanity."

"Okay," I whispered. "Thank you."

He smiled. "Anytime."

Then he was gone and I was left to the car, to my thoughts, to my worry.

Because Ro still wasn't picking up.

I shoved my fear that I'd irrevocably broken us away, got out of the car, and started pacing back and forth by the open door, unable to sit still, needing to do *something*, even if it was just walking five feet forward, turning, and then five feet back.

Another plane pulled in on the next tarmac, and parked, and I sighed, glancing away from it, gaze searching for my promised crew.

I'd been so fucking stupid, and now I was stuck here and Ro was—

Walking across the tarmac.

"What?" I whispered, gaze whipping back to the plane that had pulled in, seeing that the stairs had been opened, its crew bustling around the aircraft.

And *Rome* was walking across the tarmac.

I gasped and didn't think, just sprinted.

Across the asphalt, toward the man I loved.

I was crying and shaking and—

I launched myself into his arms.

He caught me—of course he did—enfolding me in his embrace, my name a benediction on his tongue, his face in my hair, his body shaking as much as mine was. "Maddie. Fuck. *Maddie.*"

"I'm sorry," I whispered. "I want us. I want you. I *love* you."

He shuddered. "Thank God. Thank *God*, baby. Because"—he pulled back, cupped my cheeks—"I lied."

My eyebrows pulled together.

He leaned down, close enough that our breaths mingled, that our eyes could only be focused on each other.

"I can't let you go, even if you want it."

"Ro," I whispered.

"I will follow you to the ends of the world, baby."

"You won't need to." I took his hands in mine, squeezed tightly. "Because I'm not leaving you. Not now. Not today. Not ever. My heart is yours to keep safe, honey, and I expect you to give me yours all the same."

His eyes closed, but not before I saw them fill with relief. "It's already on a platter and extended your direction."

"I love you," I whispered.

"I love *you*."

I squeezed his hands again. "I'm sorry you had to come all the way to Germany to hear those words."

He smiled. "I'm not."

"What? Why?" My eyes went wide.

He released my hands, but slid his arms around me, drawing me against him when he murmured, "I spent weeks trying to find the perfect moment to tell you I love you." He shook his head. "And I don't think I could have found a better time or place to get those words back."

"Even with the side of a twelve-hour plane ride?"

His smile grew. "Definitely."

My eyes widened. "Why?"

He took my hand, drew me toward his plane. "Because I already have another crew on standby to fly us home." A tug and I was in front of him, ascending the stairs. "Which means we get twelve hours to celebrate."

"Actually," I said. "We have thirteen."

He leaned around me, brows up in question.

"The jet stream," I whispered.

Grinning, he nudged me forward and fully onto the plane, hustling me back to the bedroom, calling out instructions to the flight crew as he went.

Then we were in the room and the door was closed—and locked—behind us.

I reached down, yanked my shirt over my head.

"God, I love the jet stream," he said, tossing me onto the bed.

I squealed, found myself naked and beneath Ro and...what seemed like only minutes later, in the air.

We took full advantage of those thirteen hours.

*Full* advantage.

And it wasn't until we were descending into San Francisco that I realized I'd just accumulated another favor that I owed Brooks Saxton.

But, with Ro's arms around me, I found I didn't care.

I was firmly on the Light Side.

# EPILOGUE

## RO, FIVE YEARS LATER

I was exhausted.

The flight had been long and my day longer, getting up before dawn, flying out to a meeting in New York, getting back on the plane as soon as it was done.

So, I'd be home for dinner.

That was Maddie's and my deal.

We'd always be home for dinner.

Something that had gotten increasingly difficult as my company grew, as her responsibilities and position within Ash's increased.

Busy.

Always so busy. Always thinking that, at some point, life would slow down.

Always knowing we were lying to ourselves.

Because slowing down wasn't our thing.

Grabbing on to life and living to the fullest was. Big jobs. Big trips. Big wedding.

Big...family.

I hit the button to close the garage door and got out of my car, moving into the house.

Smelling the delicious scent of Maddie's cooking.

Sometimes it was order in. Other times Jack or I cooked. Or we had a big family dinner with my siblings and their crazy, busy families. Sometimes, if we were going to be particularly busy, we had a chef come in and make food for us.

Spoiled? Yes.

But if it took the pressure off so my woman could work and love her family and not be stressed out before her head hit the pillow then I was good with it.

Plus, I was rich.

I could afford it.

Rolling my eyes at myself, I walked through the mudroom and into the kitchen.

Glimpsing the sight that never failed to freeze me in my tracks.

Maddie at the sink, washing up some dishes. Jack at the stove, stirring a pot. Jamie, our daughter, on a stool and using a plastic knife to cut up something for the brother she adored—usually something Jack didn't actually need for the recipe, but something that he accepted and added graciously anyway.

Because if he'd been a good kid five years ago...

He was fucking *incredible* now.

They didn't see me.

They never did.

Not our twins—Athena and Daisy—in their highchairs, food smeared on their cheeks. Not Jamie or Jack. Not Maddie as she dried her hands on a towel and turned to supervise, the curve of her pregnant belly illustrating *exactly* how crazy we were.

And how serious I was about life not slowing down any time soon.

Jamie said something and Jack laughed, the twins joining in, not understanding the joke, but just wanting to laugh because everyone else was.

Laughter.

Food.

Family.

My heart squeezed.

All I'd ever wanted was right here in this room...

Including the first living, breathing creature to realize I'd come into the house.

Freckles, our corgi, saw me. For the record, I didn't name her, and I never would have picked the moniker, but somehow, after all these years, Freckles fit.

Freckles lifted her head, eyes cataloging every human in the room, keeping track of them all as she got up and trotted my way, panting happily at my feet. I bent, scratched her, knowing that her cuddles were soon to be interrupt—

"Dad!"

—ed.

One more pat and I was straightening, catching a leaping Jaime, hugging her tight and looking over her head, at the woman who owned my heart but had always made room inside her own for our ever-growing family.

Making sure no one ever felt left out.

Making sure everyone felt loved.

I'd always thought that I needed to be the one doing all the catching, all the saving, all the protecting.

The people—and corgi—in this room had taught me differently.

Starting with a stubborn mini-me.

Continuing with a stubborn, blue-eyed brunette.

And a stubborn brown-haired toddler and blue-eyed twins and...another son, who was six days overdue.

My messy, beautiful family.

My small slice of fantasy.

My *everything*.

I put Jaime down, ruffled Jack's hair, kissed the twins on their heads.

But when I reached Maddie, she pulled back before our lips could touch.

I frowned, opened my mouth—

And then I felt it.

The splash on my ankles.

"Is that—?"

Her eyes widened and she glanced down, my eyes following hers, seeing that, yes indeed, her water had just broken.

She sighed, shook her head, mouth curving. "Such a Hutchins."

Grinning, she rose on tiptoe, kissed me long and deep and slow, letting me taste her smile, her happiness. Then she slowly pulled back, her hand going to her belly.

"It's time to add to our big, beautiful life."

———

## BROOKS

She was beautiful.

She was walking toward me in a wedding dress, crisp white and fitted in a way that mixed innocence and sin.

Sleek fabric clinging to breasts I'd dreamed about, hips I'd imagined grasping as I thrust deep, splitting on mid-thigh to give a glimpse of silken skin.

Mine.

*Mine.*

The thought ricocheted through me so violently, I knew.

*Knew.*

The truth.

The reality.

The...future.

But by then, she was there.

Her bright blue eyes glimmering with love and hope, with tears of happiness.

She...was beauty and good and...

I was a monster.

I was going to destroy her.

Her hand found mine and she stepped close, fingers tightening in that soft way of hers. Plump lips painted pink. Freckles softened by her makeup. Lashes that rested gently on her cheeks when she slept.

"Dearly beloved we are gathered here today to..."

I nearly jumped out of my skin at the soft female voice standing between us, holding a book even though it was clear she had her spiel memorized, even down to the timing of pauses, waiting for chuckles or laughter or whatever feedback an officiant normally received from a wedding ceremony.

But there weren't rows and rows of chairs, filled with loving family and friends.

There weren't many voices to lend their approval of the quiet jokes and idioms.

Just two stoic witnesses—my bodyguards, who I trusted with my life...and hers.

Mountains behind us.

A narrow swathe of pine trees, their branches intertwined to form a canopy overhead.

A peaceful place.

*Her* place.

I was going to ruin that too.

*Boom!*

Thunder rattled through the air, vibrated through my chest, my stomach. Pine needles shook in the window. Clouds gathered, clinging together, darkening the sky.

Fat, wet drops began plopping to the ground, darkening the dirt, splattering onto my head, my suit.

Her dress.

Laughter in the air—the sound that had so captivated me, that had drawn me to this sweet, beautiful, *innocent* woman against every single reservation that I had.

It wasn't a sound I deserved to hear.

It was a sound I wouldn't hear.

Not ever again.

Not after this.

Briar laughed as the drops began gathering on her skin like glittering diamonds.

The officiant stopped, closed the book in her hands, glancing at them then up at the clouds. "Should we stop?"

"No!" Briar said again, slipping one hand from mine and extending it, droplets splashing onto her thumb. "I love the rain!" she cried, tilting her head back, embracing the drops as they fell onto her hair, darkening the blond stands, straightening the curls, soaking the fabric of her dress.

A pause from the officiant. Then she reopened her book.

Briar's eyes slid to mine, buoyant with joy. "This is perfect," she whispered as thunder boomed again

Lightning cut across the sky.

Rain continued to fall.

"Perfect," she whispered again, her damp palm coming to mine, fingers wrapping tight again.

No.

It wasn't.

Before I could say something, could find the strength to pull my fingers from hers, the officiant continued.

"Do you, Brooks Saxton, take this woman to be your lawfully wedded wife, to live together in matrimony, to love her, comfort her, honor and keep her in sickness and in health, in sorrow and in joy, to have and to hold, from this day forward, as long as you both shall—"

"I don't."

The words were ripped from my soul.

Spat into the air.

Shock reverberated back.

From the officiant.

From the witnesses.

From *Briar*.

"I don't," I repeated.

Fingers convulsed around mine. "You're supposed to say *I do*."

My lungs seized. "No," I whispered. "I'm not."

"Brooks—"

I slipped my hands from hers. It wasn't easy, not when she was clinging so fiercely. Not when she was looking at me like...

I couldn't allow that thought to form, couldn't allow the words to coalesce in my mind.

I might do something that was worse than this.

I might...stay.

"I don't," I said for a third time.

Though this time I paired it with putting distance between us, enough and so quickly that I saw it break off a little chunk of that innocence, that sweetness, that essence that was purely Briar.

It fell aside.

Gone.

Forever.

"You're supposed to say *I do*," Briar said again, more fiercely.

I shook my head, committed her face to memory, knew I needed to hold it tight, knew it was the only memory of her I deserved.

Then I turned away. Turned from the sputtering of the officiant, turned from the shattering beauty.

I moved toward Thanes and Max. They'd been with me from the beginning.

Long enough to not question anything.

"Max." I flicked my eyes in the direction of Briar.

He nodded...just as footsteps echoed across the earth, louder than the rain, which was coming down in sheets, drenching him, the earth.

Briar.

"Brooks!"

Max had been with me a long time.

Long enough to step behind me, to intercept Briar before she could touch me.

*"Brooks!"*

I started walked.

*Kept* walking.

Down along the narrow winding trail, the faint imprint in earthen ground that Briar knew by heart.

Her place.

Our place.

I kept walking...

Out of her life.

I thought forever.

I was wrong.

———

Thank you for reading! I hope you loved spending time in the Billionaire's Club world with me! It's time to transition to a new group of billionaire bad boys...starting with Brooks Saxton in RUTHLESS BILLIONAIRE! **I broke the woman who loved me...and I didn't care...**

CLICK HERE TO READ RUTHLESS BILLIONAIRE NOW>

And if you enjoyed BAD BUSINESS, don't miss the Gold Hockey series. It begins with the over 400 five-star-reviewed BLOCKED! **The more she falls for Stefan, the more she risks her career...**

*"Off-the-charts hot, smexy scenes with one of the best book boyfriends I have come across!"* —Amazon reviewer

DOWNLOAD BLOCKED FOR FREE >

---

**If you enjoy my series, considering supporting me on PATREON! Get access to early releases, bonus content, character art, audiobooks, special edition covers, swag, and much more!**

CLICK HERE TO SUPPORT ME>

I so appreciate your help in spreading the word about my books, including sharing with friends! Please leave a review on your favorite book site!

You can also join my Facebook group, the Fabinators, for exclusive giveaways and sneak peeks of future books.

SIGN UP FOR ELISE FABER'S NEWSLETTER HERE: https://www.elisefaber.com/newsletter

---

Hate missing Elise's new releases? Love contests, exclusive excerpts and giveaways?

Then signup for Elise's newsletter here!

www.elisefaber.com/newsletter

---

And join Elise's fan group, the Fabinators (https://www.facebook.com/groups/fabinators) for insider information, sneak peaks at new releases, and fun freebies! Hope to see you there!

---

I so appreciate your help in spreading the word about my books, including sharing with friends! Please leave a review on your favorite book site!

# BILLIONAIRE'S CLUB

Bad Night Stand

Bad Breakup

Bad Husband

Bad Hookup

Bad Divorce

Bad Fiancé

Bad Boyfriend

Bad Blind Date

Bad Wedding

Bad Engagement

Bad Bridesmaid

Bad Swipe

Bad Girlfriend

Bad Best Friend

Bad Rebound

Bad Romance

Bad Business

# Also by Elise Faber

Blocked

Backhand

Boarding

Benched

Breakaway

Breakout

Checked

Coasting

Centered

Charging

Caged

Crashed

A Gold Christmas

Cycled

Caught

Cap

Covered

Crushed

Changed

Scored

*Breakers Hockey (all stand alone)*

<u>Broken</u>

<u>Boldly</u>

<u>Breathless</u>

<u>Ballsy</u>

<u>Bewitched</u>

Blowout

Breathe

Blazed

## *Sierra Hockey Series*

Over the Line

The Big Skate

Caught from Behind

On the Fly

## *Rush Hockey Trilogy #1*

Big Puck Energy

Filthy Puckboy

So Pucking Over It

## *Rush Hockey Trilogy #2*

Love, Pucks, and Other Stories

All's Fair in Pucks and War

No Pucks Lost Between Us

## *Eagles Hockey Series (all stand alone)*

Broken Laces

## *Love, Action, Camera (all stand alone)*

Dotted Line

Action Shot

Close-Up

End Scene

Meet Cute

**_Love After Midnight_ (all stand alone)**

Rum And Notes

Virgin Daiquiri

On The Rocks

Sex On The Seats

**_Life Sucks Series_ (all stand alone)**

Train Wreck

Hot Mess

Dumpster Fire

Clusterf*@k

FUBAR

Perfect Storm

Free Fall

Lost Cause

**_Roosevelt Ranch Series_ (all stand alone, series complete)**

Disaster at Roosevelt Ranch

Heartbreak at Roosevelt Ranch

Collision at Roosevelt Ranch

Regret at Roosevelt Ranch

Desire at Roosevelt Ranch

**_Phoenix Series_ (read in order)**

Phoenix Rising

Dark Phoenix

Phoenix Freed

**_Phoenix: LexTal Chronicles_ (rereleasing soon, stand alone, Phoenix**

**world)**

From Ashes

In Flames

To Smoke

*KTS Series (all stand alone, series complete)*

Riding The Edge

Crossing The Line

Leveling The Field

Scorching The Earth

*Cocky Heroes World*

Tattooed Troublemaker

# About the Author

*USA Today* bestselling author, Elise Faber, loves chocolate, Star Wars, Harry Potter, and hockey (the order depending on the day and how well her team -- the Sharks! -- are playing). She and her husband also play as much hockey as they can squeeze into their schedules, so much so that their typical date night is spent on the ice. Elise changes her hair color more often than some people change their socks, loves sparkly things, and is the mom to two exuberant boys. She lives in Northern California. Connect with her in her Facebook group, the Fabinators or find more information about her books at www.elisefaber.com.

[f] facebook.com/elisefaberauthor

[a] amazon.com/author/elisefaber

[BB] bookbub.com/profile/elise-faber

[O] instagram.com/elisefaber

[g] goodreads.com/elisefaber

[P] pinterest.com/elisefaberwrite